WERE WAR

WERE WAR

WEREWITCH™ BOOK FOUR

RENÉE JAGGÉR

LMBPN Publishing
PMB 196, 2540 South Maryland Pkwy
Las Vegas, NV 89109

First US Release, September 2020
eBook ISBN: 978-1-64971-154-0
Print ISBN: 978-1-64971-155-7

CHAPTER ONE

A young woman in jeans and boots and a flannel shirt tied at the waist stood upon a brambly hillock amidst a landscape drawn from a disturbing dream. No wind seemed to stir the gnarled branches of the ancient black trees, nor did the slate-colored clouds move much across the deep purple sky, yet it seemed like a breeze lifted the girl's brown hair.

She looked out across the boggy, mist-shrouded wastes of the Other, the parallel world formed of the residue of other worlds' magic.

Here I am, she thought. *I was told that things would start getting better. That being a shaman would make my life less dangerous, and that I'd finally have the chance to get the hell away from trouble for a while.*

A dark shape like the silhouette of a huge bat or a pterodactyl streaked across the sky, but she barely registered its presence.

How was I supposed to know that the trials to become an apprentice would be a million times more likely to kill me than anything else I've done? And I've had people trying to take my head off for a while now.

She sighed and steeled herself as the hulking figure across the hill from her raised his hands, which were crackling with the power of deadly spells.

Magic, she concluded. *Ain't it a bitch?*

The man attacked.

At first, a vertical line of dark purple light appeared in front of him, as though it were about to streak toward her in the form of a fiery beam, but then it spread to either side, protecting him as a shield.

Simultaneously, a crackling bolt appeared *behind* her. She'd expected some kind of trickery, though, and her sharp lycanthropic senses picked up the change in the air in an instant. She launched herself straight up and let the bolt pass under her. It struck the man's shield instead, where it sparked massively before fizzling out.

While airborne, Bailey summoned her counterattack— a gout of flame that erupted from the earth beneath her opponent's feet, combined with similar blasts that came in from the sides just above his head. The idea was to catch him as he jumped away from the first strike.

Instead, he shielded himself from below, dissipating the flames so they resembled a giant orange flower, then rolled forward. His coat started to smoke but didn't ignite as the horizontal firestorms crashed and exploded just above the point where he'd been standing.

"Shit!" Air rushed past Bailey, and the ground sailed up to meet her. She fought its pull, slowing her descent and coming to rest in the upper branches of a tree. By the time her feet found their perch, she was tossing a spiraling mass of lightning and ice at the tall man.

He spun to face her and caught the blast with one hand while hurling electrified plasma at her with the other.

Although her body was strained, Bailey's mind felt lucid, focused, almost calm. The Other naturally tended to impose limits on magical expenditure, sapping the power of spells, but for a sufficiently experienced channeler, there were ways around it.

Distributing her energy as efficiently as she could, she caught the man's plasma bolt and threw it back. She also maintained her hold on the mass of death hovering in the air just in front of his position, trying to force it back to engulf him.

The two concentrations of arcane power blended, eventually becoming a sort of spherical vortex of multicolored light and matter that bulged and twisted as each combatant sought to gain control of it. Random lances of blended elements shot out from the central mass here and there.

One went safely below Bailey but struck the tree she stood in. She clamped down on her sense of alarm as the blackened wood exploded in a shower of fragments, dropping her to the ground.

Striving not to get too self-conscious about it, she kept control of the magical vortex even as she fell and rolled. Her opponent moved it back toward her, but she didn't lose it.

Once she was able to stand back up, she sent a rippling tremor through the earth toward the man, knocking him off balance, although he maintained his hold, too. He looked at her, his eyes visible even through the storm of magic.

Marcus raised a hand. "Hold," he commanded, the terrible force of his spells dwindling and growing quiet.

Bailey allowed her attacks and defenses to dissipate as well, although she remained on guard. She might have to renew them at any moment, since that, too, might be part of the tests.

But no further assault came. "Let us call it a draw," said Marcus.

Drawing ragged breaths but unbowed, Bailey put her fists on her hips. "I guess that's one way of admitting I'd have beat your ass sooner or later if we'd kept going."

The tall man almost smiled. "Perhaps you might have, just maybe. But for now, let's just say that I feel you've continued to progress at the pace you should. We've done all we can for now."

"Yeah, yeah," the girl shot back, then her face broke into a grin. "That's what they all say."

Marcus just beckoned for her to follow him. They trudged down the hill and through a brambly, swampy patch of woods. Wraiths made of material darkness hovered in the shadows between the trees, watching them but hesitant to act. The creatures must have sensed the massive power of the two visitors and known they would fail to claim a victim if they attacked.

Time did not pass in the Other as it did in the mortal world. Still, it seemed like only a few minutes had gone by when the pair reached the edge of a murky lake with mist hovering around its shores.

Bailey sighed with relief. For a second, she'd worried it

was the Pool of Dark Reflections, where she'd beheld two nightmare visions and seen four witches die. But it was another lake, just an ordinary body of water.

To the extent that anything here was "ordinary."

She sat down on a raised bank of sand and silt the color of graphite, and Marcus piled up a mass of sticks and branches he gathered from the tangled forest. Then, with a couple of quick motions, he coaxed a campfire into existence.

It burned steadily and with less smoke than Bailey would have guessed, given the dampness of the place. She rubbed her arms and closed her eyes in satisfaction, glad for the relief it brought from the realm's clammy chill.

The shaman lowered himself to ground on the other side of the blaze.

"Let us talk," he began, "about how you've been doing. And about the further course of your training. Now that you know who I am, I'm sure you can appreciate that I have good reasons for putting you through all this."

A slight tingle worked its way along the young woman's back. She still could scarcely believe that the man she'd thought was an obscure shaman from somewhere in the wilds of the Cascade Mountains was in truth Fenris, god of wolves, father of all Weres.

But she'd seen his true form, and so had the Eastmoor Pack, who even now were probably spreading the word all throughout Oregon, if not the entire western half of North America.

"Yeah," she replied, unable to keep the obvious fatigue out of her voice. "It's rough, but I understand. Mostly, anyway."

The shaman nodded. "You've progressed a great deal in terms of power and control. You wouldn't have been able to defeat those Venatori witches if you hadn't, but there's still more to learn. Now we need to focus on building your stamina."

She gave a slow nod; that was about what she'd guessed. And, she had to admit, what she'd been afraid to hear. It was hard to go much beyond the point to which she'd already been pushed.

Marcus went on, "That is why we've been at this for so long—almost two days back in your world—with so little rest, and in the taxing environment of the Other. This will train you to deal with even the most difficult of all circumstances so that lesser challenges will not be so intimidating."

Some days ago, he'd said something that had stuck with her. Practicing magic in the Other, where expulsions of arcane power were suppressed and weakened, was like doing aerobic training with an oxygen deprivation mask. It forced you to become more efficient.

She thought she'd broken through the barriers the place imposed, but being in here for this long, she was feeling the old strain again.

"The Other," he continued, "is also a safe place to train. Not so much for us, but for other people, as well as the land and woods. Your responsibility as a shaman is to protect and guide your pack, and to be a good steward to the integrity of the land. That means no wanton destruction unless absolutely necessary, and measured responses rather than reckless ones."

He stared at her for a moment after making that last comment.

She grimaced. It was no secret that she was impetuous. She sometimes overreacted to threats and challenges, and that she didn't think too hard about safety or collateral damage when the shit hit the fan.

That tendency had been with her long before she'd known she had magic. Everyone in town knew that Bailey Nordin wouldn't shy away from a fight, a dare, or an opportunity to drive like crazy over rough roads and worse terrain.

"I understand," she stated.

"Good." The man looked into the hazy distance of the deep-violet sky. "The shaman and the werewitch are unlike the common lycanthrope in more ways than one. Being able to channel the arcane gives you the ability to go farther and longer in fights, mustering higher levels of force for prolonged periods. It's a kind of endurance that goes beyond what even the strongest of the regular shifters can achieve."

She felt like she was already at that point but didn't voice her protest for now. She just let him speak.

"A truly adept shaman," he elaborated, "is of only limited use if their abilities come forth in short spurts, like a puff of smoke that looks impressive but dissipates soon after. Power, control, and endurance. The third is what we're now focused on. It's one of several things you still require."

She squinted at him through the tongues of fire. "What are the others?"

Waving a hand, he said, "We'll come to those in time."

Bailey sighed and looked down at the wood, where red coals were forming. It seemed just then that the campfire separated her from her teacher by a distance of far more than a few feet. The expanse of the Other around here seemed to cut her off from *everyone* else as well. For the first time in a long time, she felt alone.

Marcus must have noticed. "You miss Roland," he declared. "He's been by your side through most of this."

"Yeah," she admitted. "I guess it's kind of stupid since he's around. He still is, right?"

The shaman nodded. "He has tasks of his own to work on. They will make him a more effective companion for you."

The implications of the word "companion" made her face flush but also brought a warm tingling sensation she wasn't prepared to deal with right now.

Instead, she asked a question. "What's his problem, anyway? I mean, what do you think the big hurdle he's trying to clear with his training right now is?"

Marcus rubbed his whiskered chin. "An inner conflict of sorts. He already has power and control, although as a wizard, the style of magic he learned was limited by his people's traditions. I'd say his big challenge is coming to terms with his ancestry, his role as a powerful male witch, and the ways in which his very existence seemed to disrupt the usual order of things in his community. In that regard, the two of you are similar."

She gave a low, snorting chuckle. "You got that right. Hell, I never asked to be special or whatever. Speaking of which, what should I work on? Endurance, yeah, but more specifically, what kinds of exercises are we gonna do next?"

The man paused. To her chagrin, he didn't give her a direct answer.

"You are not even an apprentice shaman yet, more of a trainee. Right now, you are passing the trials to determine your eligibility for beginning your apprenticeship. There are sophisticated physical and spiritual trials to go through. At this point, you have fulfilled the prerequisite of proving that you're not going to kill yourself with your magic."

Her gut clenched. She'd somehow thought she was already well into the process of becoming a shaman.

Why wasn't he clearer with me about that? Is that part of the trials, too? Seeing how well I take disappointment?

Marcus continued, "As a natural werewitch, you have the potential. But with that much raw power…well, those who train you or interact with you don't want to be blown apart, nor do they particularly want you to blow yourself to kingdom come. That danger is passing as you gain control. What comes next, though, will be even harder."

Suddenly she was annoyed with all the ominous crap. She recalled that she'd already done stuff that was truly incredible.

"Okay," she said, her voice a little stronger, "bring it on. What's next?"

The shaman tossed a stick into the fire. "The spiritual quests you'll have to undergo will tax you in ways you might not expect. They will make you question who and what you are, and the questions you find yourself asking will not always be the kind that you want to hear the answers to. They will strip away your illusions—the layers of psychological defense mechanisms and self-justifications we often employ—leaving only the raw and naked core of your personality. It's a process that not everyone comes back from with their mind still intact. Some have gone mad."

She sat holding his gaze and digesting his words but did not respond since what he'd just said was only half of what awaited her.

Marcus proceeded to the second half. "The physical trials, on the other hand, are designed to threaten your life, abusing your body in ways such that it has no choice but to regrow stronger than it's ever been. It will prove how much you're willing to go through—strain, deprivation, exhaustion, and pain—all of which are a preview for the challenges posed to shamans."

Something crazy deep within the girl's brain, primitive and ferocious, took over and she grinned, showing her teeth.

"You line 'em up," she stated, "and I'll knock 'em down. I've kicked the ass of everything else that's come my way so far. No reason to think it won't be the same way with the rest."

Marcus smiled back, but his expression was far more subdued. "Good. You're certainly not lacking in courage or determination."

He stood up with a nimbleness and speed that belied his age. Or would, if he were a man instead of a deity in human form.

"Stay where you are," he told her, "and rest. Think. Meditate. Roland might be back soon. How soon depends on him, of course. I have an errand or two to run. I'll return for you, though."

She shrugged. "Okay." It was customary by now for the shaman to excuse himself whenever he saw fit.

The girl half-watched him through the flames as he strode off into the dark woods, making no more sound than a lean wolf on the hunt.

The young man was only twenty-six, but the hard lines of his face, along with his shaved head—he'd likely started balding prematurely—made him look ten or twelve years older. He was fit and powerful of build, though, and his small black chin-beard gave him a curiously regal or authoritative appearance that was in no way detracted from by his sleeveless shirt, tattooed arms, or ripped jeans. He seemed to be a kind of redneck statesman in the making.

As well as a shaman in the making.

"You must understand," Marcus stated, his voice low but steely-firm, "that I wouldn't have come all this way and gone under and around your master's authority if it wasn't important. The fact that I'm speaking to you now is evidence of the magnitude of the threat we're facing."

Nicolas Jezak nodded with his chin. "Okay," he replied in a voice almost as gravelly as Marcus', though a half-octave higher. "What is it, then? I gotta get back to training shortly."

The two of them stood in a sunlit glade in the woods just outside the town of Shashka, Oregon, in the mountain foothills southeast of Salem. Like most Were towns in the region, it lay off the proverbial beaten path, located on a road seldom frequented by outsiders or long-distance travelers.

It was about a two-hour drive from Bailey's hometown of Greenhearth. Of course, Marcus had ways of getting there far more quickly.

The older man paused for a few seconds for dramatic effect, as though trying to decide how to approach the subject or how much he should reveal. "Have you heard of a Were named Bailey Nordin?"

There was a slight tensing of the muscles along Nick's square jaw. "Yeah, I have. Pretty sure every Were in the Pacific Northwest has, if not the whole goddamn continent by now."

"Yes," Marcus responded. "I see. Then you've likely heard that no one is quite sure what to make of her. Some think she's a hero, others think she's dangerous. No one knows what to believe. Do they?"

The apprentice shaman considered the inquiry. "I guess not. I don't like most of what I've heard, but I got my own shit to deal with in the meantime. I figured I'd wait and see how things pan out."

Marcus stood looking at Nick but deliberately held off on speaking for a moment, waiting just long enough to make the pause awkward. "I do not think that would be a good idea," he intoned. His face was grave.

"Why not?" Nick asked. He seemed suspicious, but probably not of the shaman.

"Because," said Marcus, "she's a hurricane in the form of a young woman. Shitstorm-category, to put it crudely. She has a lot of power but little self-control or self-discipline. A loose cannon. It is my opinion, after observing her for a while now, that she's a danger to the entire community. She has good publicity among some groups, yes, but she has been directly or indirectly responsible for multiple deaths and far too much needless destruction."

He shook his head while looking into the distance.

Nick narrowed his eyes. "Okay. Well, thanks for the warning. Right now I'm focused on doing the stuff my teacher wants, but if she comes around here, I'll—"

"Have you considered," Marcus interrupted, "taking the initiative? It's expected of all young shamans at some point. Your teacher might be impressed if you were to, on your own time, deal with a threat to all Weres before that threat had time to gather too much momentum."

The younger man considered. A slight twitch of his eyebrow suggested that he was surprised, even mildly shocked by the idea, but it took root in his brain. Slowly, a hungry look of ambition spread across his face.

"I hadn't considered that," he confessed, "but maybe I should."

Marcus nodded. "Yes. And the sooner you reach a decision, the better."

CHAPTER TWO

Bailey's ears, ever sensitive, picked up the soft sound of footsteps approaching. She perked up—not afraid, but alert. It was likely her visitor would turn out to be either Marcus or Roland, but it would be foolish to leap to a conclusion.

She had, after all, been attacked in the Other twice by hostile magical forces.

First by the trio of Seattle witches who wanted Roland for themselves. Second, by a task force sent by the dreaded Venatori, the fanatical European order of sorceresses who viewed Bailey as a threat to their arcane hegemony.

As the footfalls drew closer, though, they started to sound familiar, and soon she recognized the tall, slim person to which they belonged.

"Hi, Roland," she called. "Marcus made a good old-fashioned campfire. Not that you'd have much experience with those since you're a city boy, but it's never too late to appreciate one."

The wizard strolled up, his frame bowed by tiredness.

his blond hair hanging lank and sweaty over the fine classical features of his face.

"Sounds great," he said. "Compared to the Pacific Northwest in the real world, this goddamn place is mind-numbingly consistent in being cold and damp and gloomy."

She smirked a bit. "Looks like you got a workout, though. You're as sweaty as if we'd been doing this shit in Texas in the middle of July."

"Something like that." He came into the glow cast by the small blaze and lowered himself to the ground, crossing his legs in front of him. "Anyway, both of us are still alive, which I guess counts as evidence that we've been doing something right in our training. Of course, it's still possible to die of exhaustion."

The girl frowned. "I don't think Marcus plans to push us *that* hard. He's trying to get the best out of us, so we have to go to our limits. I can't see him being stupid enough to kill us with a training mistake. Especially considering, you know, who he really is."

She swallowed.

Roland shook his head in an unhurried, deliberate way. He hadn't been present when Marcus had revealed himself as a Norse deity made flesh.

"If it wasn't for Freya manifesting a few weeks back," he remarked, "there's no way in hell I would believe that. No offense. I trust you, but I would have guessed he was just some especially powerful caster putting on a very convincing illusion. Freya was no illusion, though, so I suppose I'm required to believe that her nephew or second cousin or whatever he is could show up at some point, too."

"Yeah," she replied. "Hell, it took me a while to accept it too, but in his true form, he was no illusion."

They sat together quietly for a couple of minutes, and Roland took her hand. She didn't object.

"So," he asked, "how did the fighting go?"

She told him, discussing how she'd mostly learned to work around the Other's limiting factors, but having to channel her power over such an extensive period of time was wearing her down.

"I fought him to a draw, though," she pointed out. "As a god, maybe he has powers I could never match no matter what, but on the level we were operating at? I held my own. Might have even been able to beat him."

The wizard smiled. He wasn't overly fond of Marcus, and he seemed to be enjoying the thought of Bailey potentially defeating him. "Good shit. If you ever win, let me know, then tell me how you did it. That way, maybe I can have the same opportunity."

She gently punched him on the arm. "Come on, he's not that bad. He's helped us a lot. Anyway, what were you getting up to at, uh, wherever it was you went?"

"Oh, you know." He waved a hand. "Things and stuff."

She scowled at him, so he sighed and went on.

"Much of what I did was less, uh, dramatic or pyrotechnic than what you were up to. More internal struggles, you might say. Visions and soul-searching and crap like that. I find that…"

He hesitated, obviously a bit uncomfortable, so Bailey didn't press him. She just looked at him, face free of judgment, and waited until he continued speaking. He'd done the same for her many times in the past.

Finally, he managed it. "I keep wondering about my heritage, the true nature of it." He gazed into the gloom beyond the fire's glow. "I have greater magical potential than usual, especially for a male in a sub-species where women are usually the more talented casters. But where does it come from? Is it just an accident of heredity? Some random combination of genetic traits that was just right for me to end up the way I have? Or is it part of something that stretches way back? I don't know. Nobody has ever talked about it."

Listening to him, Bailey realized that she had the same questions about him and also about herself. Werewitches were a rare occurrence in recent history.

"And if it is some sort of legacy that's coming out of the dim shadows of history or something, is it the source of all my goddamn problems? Would I still have had Shannon and her lackeys after me, not to mention the Venatori now, and possibly the Agency as well?"

After a second, he turned to look at her and noticed the slightly curdled and uncomfortable expression on her face.

"Of course," he added, "the fact that all this stuff *has* happened means I met you, also. So that's the upside."

She smiled. "Nice save."

"But," he went on, "at first I thought, I'm dragging you into all this. You put yourself in harm's way partially to help me, and therefore I had a responsibility to protect you from the witches or whoever else might try to retaliate against us. But now, with you as this big, badass were-witch-shaman and the pupil of a frickin' *god*, it's like you don't really *need* me to protect you. I'm glad to be here—I practically live with your family now, after all—but sometimes I wonder why I *am* here. Like, is there still some purpose I'm supposed to serve, a role I have to play?"

Bailey didn't have any easy answers to the existential aspects of the questions he'd posed. She was burdened enough by answering similar ones about her own situation.

Still, there was one thing she could tell him.

"Well, even with all my new powers," she observed, "I woulda got my ass kicked by the Venatori without your help. Even with two of us, both strong channelers now, it was a damn close fight. I'd say we're about equal. And we're in it together."

The wizard relaxed; his vibe and demeanor grew warmer. "Yes, that's true," he conceded. "And thanks for saying so."

She gave his hand a gentle squeeze. "No problem."

He exhaled. "Still, I feel like Marcus intends for me to make some kind of breakthrough almost as big as the ones you've made, rather than simply honing the skills I already have. Is it vain of me to want that? To want to get better to, I don't know, grow into my identity? Or should I just take things as they come?"

Bailey shrugged. "Not saying I blame you for wondering, but try not to worry about it too much. Whatever happens, I'm just glad you're with me through it. Well, most of it."

"Fair enough." The warmth coming off of him ratcheted up a notch. Clearly, he was feeling better just for having got all that off his chest.

It was making her think, though. "For my part? I'm not gonna lie, I'm…worried, I guess, about all these trials that Marcus—Fenris—has in mind. When I was with him, I acted all cocky about it—no big deal, I'll kick ass and so on. But deep down, I dunno. I think I can do it. It's just killing me that I don't know what's coming. Or what's expected of me."

"Makes sense." The wizard nodded.

She continued, "I'd rather be doing something. Like, if there's a job to get done, I want to hear about it so I can get to work. If there's something I have to face, then bring it on so I can deal with it. All these ominous warnings about vague stuff that *might* happen? Ugh. Not my favorite thing."

Roland tapped his lips. "Hmm. Well, if you want something to face, we could always summon some of those awful shadow-wraith things from one of the pools. The Other just loves to spit those bastards out at inopportune times. And you'd get more practice in! Just what we both need."

She groaned, but the sound transformed into a laugh. "Yeah, yeah, shut up." She elbowed him in the ribs.

"Ow."

In the ancient city of Lyon in east-central France, there lay a small plaza that was closed off from the rest of the metropolis and the general public, even though the location and design were sufficiently inconspicuous that it didn't attract much attention. It fronted a nondescript office building thirteen stories tall that was linked to an old mansion by stone walls and covered walkways and separated by gardens and courtyards.

The mansion was used for ceremonial or festive occasions, but today, various women were gathering there for business. Therefore, they convened on the top floor of the modern building.

There were thirteen of them, many from France and the Low Countries, and some from elsewhere in Europe. They comprised the ruling council of the Venatori Order.

Twelve sat at the sides of the long table, six each to the left and right. The room was state of the art and lacked no convenience they might need, yet was somehow sparse and austere. The one concession to lushness was the reddish-purple lighting.

Most of them preferred the quainter environs of the mansion. Meeting here, in this stark and almost masculine environment, only emphasized the importance of their affairs.

Madame Daria Gregorovia, a woman of sixty-four from Ajaccio in Corsica, was the current Grandmistress of the Order. Even for a meeting of this type, she wore the traditional dark burgundy robes, with the hood pulled over her tightly-coiffed silver hair. Rings glittered on her long fingers, and she seldom blinked. The other chairs were modern black leather, but hers, at the head of the table, was of antique rosewood.

"Ladies," she began in French, "all of you by now have heard the news from America. While enough of a concern to merit the dispatch of a squad of operatives, it is now clear that this matter requires our *full* and *undivided* attention."

Slow nods went around the table.

"My thanks," the Grandmistress went on, "to those of you who had to travel here on short notice from as far away as Dublin, Inverness, Palermo, Dubrovnik, and St. Petersburg." She gestured in turn to the sorceress from each of the cities she'd mentioned, and the witches bowed their heads in response.

When first the Order had formally incorporated, France had been the agreed-upon country in which to headquarter. However, it had taken some time before they'd settled upon Lyon.

At first, some witches, particularly those native to southern France, had suggested Albi, from whence originated the Cathar movement, or Avignon, the seat of the "second Pope" during that controversy within the Catholic Church. Many had appreciated the symbolic value of either place, but ultimately those locations were deemed too hard to access. Thus, something farther north and east was chosen for the benefit of their members from elsewhere on the continent.

"Grandmistress," inquired Madame Natalie MacLachlan, a strawberry-blonde from the aforementioned Inverness who was the youngest witch on the council, "I heard that the entire squad we sent to the United States was wiped out. Is this true?"

The older woman at the head of the table grimaced. "All were either captured by the American authorities or killed. I would prefer to disguise the truth of such a catastrophe, but there would be no use in doing so. Not even I could have predicted the opposition they would face. Madame Lavonne was skilled enough, but she clearly underestimated her target. Hence, the urgency of this meeting."

Brief comments of assent and acknowledgment went around the chamber. Madame Gregorovia could sense which of them were subtly hostile and perhaps questioned the quality of her leadership, but she had little doubt she would win them over soon. Certainly after the mission was complete, and perhaps even by the end of today's conference.

"In response to our initial failure," she continued, 'I have authorized swift and decisive action to contain the threat and neutralize the so-called werewitch, Bailey Nordin."

A few of them looked skeptical, probably because neutralizing Nordin had been the goal of the first expedition. Most nodded their enthusiasm.

Before bothering to proceed with the discussion, Gregorovia pressed a button before her to summon drinks. A moment later, the door opened, and a pair of male servants clad like traditional butlers came in with bottles of excellent local wine, along with fine crystal glasses. They poured swiftly, then excused themselves without a word.

The ladies all drank. It was customary to complete a full draught, followed by a moment's appreciation, before resuming business.

Gregorovia was the one to break the silence, of course. "The task ahead is challenging, but we have dealt with greater threats in the past. Our great Order has persisted throughout the centuries, despite unending hostility from innumerable foes."

"Exactly," quipped MacLachlan, her tone a little too arrogant for the elder witches' liking. "And this Nordin person is just one rustic girl. I'm surprised she hasn't already been neutralized."

Madame Dorleac, second in seniority to the Grandmistress, spread a hand before her and added a comment on the one issue no one really wanted to discuss.

"There are also the rumors that the Nordin girl is now being mentored by a god," she stated. She deliberately allowed the words to weigh heavily in the air, oppressing them all with the implications.

MacLachlan jeered. "That's blithering nonsense. That gossip came from the lycanthrope community, did it not? They're a backward, ignorant people, especially in the Americas, combining the worst elements of peasants from the medieval period with the barbaric frontier settlers who first invaded that particular landmass."

Gregorovia leveled her eyes at the other witch in an expression that wasn't quite a glare but nevertheless shut her up.

"There is a disturbance in the astral plane and beyond, young Madame, and it seems to have been following that girl around of late. Great powers are converging on her. The truth of what has transpired remains to be seen, but a magical intelligence of lower or middle deity strength is not impossible. To rule out the notion altogether would be to make the same mistake Lavonne made—underestimating what we face."

Grim silence set in. MacLachlan's face was stony. Her inner thoughts were undoubtedly rebellious, at least for the moment, but she gave no protest.

Dorleac spoke again. "That annoyingly opaque American institution, the one that calls itself simply 'the Agency,' is now involved as well. Their personnel were the ones who captured the witches who survived the fight. They will likely use their clout with the American government to try to seal the country against further meddling by us. Butting heads with them could lead to an international incident. Much scrutiny of us and our activities—"

"Agreed," Gregorovia interrupted, talking swiftly to head off any lapse in confidence among her followers. "And we are already accounting for that. The force we send next will be large and powerful. But it will also enter the country via a long detour, rather than the more direct route we used last time. And we shall take great care to ensure that their presence and their movements are in the open. There are, of course, ways to effect this."

"Good," MacLachlan replied at once. "The last thing we need is an all-out bloody war with the shifters and the Men in Black or whatever they call themselves at the same time. We'll need someone competent to lead the expedition, obviously."

Gregorovia smiled. "Obviously. Hence, you were our first choice, Madame MacLachlan, and still are. Handpick your assistants from among our lower ranks. You are first to assess the situation, using your best judgment as to whether it is wise to act, and how to act, and when. Move against her only when you can do so without making things even more of a mess than they already are. Surely you're up to the task? I would hope you are since you will be departing in two days' time."

The Scotswoman's face momentarily lost its confidence. Then she inhaled, and her swagger was back.

"Of course," she agreed. "Best decision you could have made. I'll deal with the little bitch-pup in record time."

Agent Townsend sat at his desk and rubbed his eyes. The dark glasses he wore at almost all times were lying on the surface, next to four thick sheaves of paperwork.

"Fucking hell," he groaned.

The reports just kept coming in. All kinds of crap, really, but the worst—and therefore the most important— was coming from Europe, where the Agency's contacts and spies were keeping a close eye on the Venatori.

They were on the move. Still, or possibly again. It didn't matter which. Given what had transpired just under two weeks ago, *anything* they did had to be treated with the utmost suspicion.

Notably, a few of their members from the peripheral parts of Europe had been seen in France. The Agency had not yet managed to figure out where their headquarters was—the place was almost certainly cloaked with layers upon layers of top-level magic—but they were pretty sure it was somewhere in the vicinity of Lyon.

And with the girl having killed a couple members of their little US task force, it seemed pretty safe to assume that the witches were *pissed*.

"Just like we predicted," he muttered under his breath. "Here comes the aftermath of Hurricane Bailey, the ultimate fuckstorm of paperwork."

Then a pang of anguish hit him, and his gut tightened. He'd said, "we," referring to him and his partner Spall. Who was now dead, the Venatori having reduced him to ash after he'd flipped out and done the same to a couple of them. They'd worked together so long, the man had been like a brother.

Hands trembling with carefully disciplined rage, he

turned to his computer, firing up the analysis programs that would allow him to collate the incoming data and narrow the possibilities to a handful of scenarios, ranked in order of likelihood.

Of course, he already had a fairly good idea of what to expect. And if—no, *when*—the shit hit the fan, he would deal with it. Take care of it. Make it go away.

Not to mention, it would be an excellent opportunity to squeeze a little payback out of the witches' hides. He'd been too busy to make the trip, but he'd insisted on calling Spall's family to inform them that the man had died in the line of duty.

Granted, fighting hostile entities was slightly outside the Agency's purview. It wasn't their mandate, and it wasn't his job. Then again, most of his job consisted of operating out of the shadows, working in the gray areas of legality and morality.

And since it sent a strong message about the consequences of fucking with America, he was pretty damn sure that revenge fell within that gray area.

Townsend took a deep breath. The computers would need a couple of minutes to run all the necessary programs, so he could relax for the time being.

To make himself feel better, he went to the room's safe, opened it, and pulled out an alien-looking weapon, clearly a firearm of some sort. It was largely composed of a silver cylinder with multiple tubes coming out of it. Spall had used one just like it in his last moments on Earth.

The agent sat down and polished the gun, just breathing in and out. He watched another screen, the one showing a handful of confirmed Venatori members walking through the front doors of one of the international terminals at Lyon–Saint Exupéry Airport, just east of the city. He saw a relatively young woman from Scotland and a couple others native to other parts of Europe.

He chuckled, although it was a grim, mirthless sound.

"If that is what they want," he remarked, patting the weapon, "then it's what they'll get."

CHAPTER THREE

Bailey and Roland had sat together by Marcus' fire, which never seemed to burn out, until both felt rested and refreshed. Time in the Other did not pass like time on Earth, and the needs of the body were also altered. They never seemed to need food or water or sleep, nor did they need to urinate or defecate. Simply waiting long enough relieved most of their exhaustion.

"Okay," Roland said at length. "I think that's long enough. Let's get up and wander around. Maybe, if we're *especially* lucky, we'll bump into good old Marcus *before* some other group of assholes randomly pops in to challenge us to yet another fight."

Bailey chortled at that. "Sounds good to me. I dunno who else would be after us, though. Those asshole Weres who were doing all the kidnapping have mostly been taken out, and I doubt they'd have the ability to come into this place. And we beat the Venatori badly enough that I think it'll be a while before they try anything else."

The wizard rubbed his eyes. "I hope you're right, Bailey. I really do."

They stood up, stretched, and yawned, almost as though rising from slumber. Bailey used magic to lift a gallon or so of water from the nearby lake and dump it on the fire to extinguish it, then she kicked apart the coals for good measure.

"Only you," Roland said, "can prevent forest fires. Good job."

"Shut up," she responded. "If the damn thicket went up in flames, I'd have to dump the entire lake onto it, and I don't feel like doing that right now."

The wizard considered that and nodded, pursing his lips to acknowledge she had a point there.

Not sure where to go, they wandered down a vague path through the woods located about halfway between where each of them had been training.

Bailey was fairly confident they weren't far from the Pool of Dark Reflections, where much of their "inner" instruction had taken place. In fact, she suspected that was where Roland had been, although she didn't bother to ask.

Around them, the trees closed in, growing denser as they moved deeper into the forest. Beneath their feet, muddy but solid earth gave way to spongy peat that retained water-filled footprints as they passed. Black shadows pooled between the trunks around them, and Bailey thought she saw movement.

Probably more wraiths, like the ones Roland had joked about summoning. The pair's abilities were advanced enough that they could fight the creatures off without too much difficulty, but they'd rather not. They kept walking at a brisk pace, trying not to show fear or pay much attention since the eerie beings were drawn to magic and seemed to somehow feed on human emotions.

A couple of the wraiths—indistinct humanoids, looking as though they were made of darkness given material form—started to drift out from between the roots and brambles just ahead of them.

Barely slowing her pace, Bailey swiped a hand at the phantasmal creatures, engulfing them in a flashing sheet of yellow fire. Howling in awful hollow voices, they stumbled back, half-melted by the heat and light.

No more of the things bothered them.

As they emerged from the trees onto an open, boggy plain, something happened that neither of them would have expected.

A portal opened, one that was completely different from the magical gateways they'd seen before. Those were like doorways of glowing amethyst-colored water, subtle and mysterious.

This one was at least the size of the door of a good-sized garage, and it seemed like it was somehow thrown open from within on hinges of blinding sunlight, disclosing a shining expanse in which a single silhouette stood.

"Whoa!" Roland exclaimed. "Who the hell is that? Don't tell me it's another—"

The figure stepped through into the Other, and its footfalls were like the ringing of giant golden bells. The light behind the portal was so bright that it made the visitor's features impossible to distinguish at first. Once the door closed, the glare dimmed, and slowly the werewitch and the wizard were able to make out the personage before them.

It was a man, or a being shaped like a man. He stood at least seven feet tall, and his lean, muscular body was so perfectly proportioned that it almost reminded Bailey of an illustration advertising a fitness program. His beauteous, symmetrical face looked like it had been carved from crystal, and incredibly saturated blue eyes sparkled above his high cheekbones. Hair the color of polished gold swept back from his brow to spill across his shoulders.

"Uh," Bailey began, "hi."

The man took another step forward, although this time the ringing-bell sound was less pronounced.

"Greetings," he opened in a smooth voice about halfway between baritone and tenor that reminded the girl of a trumpet. His demeanor was not threatening, even though, as she now grasped, he was dressed for battle.

Namely, he wore a gold-hued suit of armor consisting of a sparkling chainmail tunic complemented by metal shoulder pauldrons, forearm bracers, and greaves. A long blue cloak flowed behind him. He also had a round shield on his back, and a single-handed sword with a short guard and a broad blade hung at his side in a scabbard of gilded leather.

Roland waved at the man, blinking, still stunned. "Greetings back. May we ask who you are?"

"I," the man replied, a calm smile on his handsome visage, "am Baldur, Norse god of light, purity, and beauty, and son of the All-father Odin."

The wizard exchanged a quick glance with Bailey. "Figures," he whispered to her, then looked back at the newcomer. "Hello, Baldur. I am technically a servant of your aunt Freya."

The deity nodded. "Yes, Roland, I know of you. And you too, Bailey. You are Fenris' vassal."

"Yeah," she replied. "I, uh, didn't know who he was until recently. I thought he was just a werewolf shaman. Well, I guess he *still is*. It's like he's the shaman-of-shamans. He's teaching Roland and me how to use our powers more responsibly."

Putting it that way, she figured, would make it sound more pleasing to the god. Phrasing along the lines of "helping us grow our powers" might come across as threatening. And right now, she didn't feel like having a being of Baldur's power regarding her as a potential enemy. The Venatori had given her enough trouble, and they were just mortals, albeit highly dangerous ones.

"Oh," Baldur stated. His demeanor was oddly bemused —almost simple or innocent—yet the whole encounter seemed pregnant with subtle threats. "I had wondered why he was interested in you. That is why I have come—to find out your reasons for training under him and to test your worth. Anyone who draws the eyes of the Aesir and Vanir must prove their mettle."

Roland let out a long sigh. "Oh, crap."

"Hold on," Bailey interjected. "Freya and Fenris have both tested us. It's not like we are infringing on your business, is it?"

Baldur seemed not to hear her words. He spoke again, still in a gentle, distant way, but now there was a colder, harder edge to his voice. "All the kin of Odin have our reasons. To command the attention of one of us is to spark the interest of the entire Norse pantheon. And perhaps some other entities, but they are beyond our purview. And here you are, a witch and a wolf. That makes you the children of my kin Freya, patron of witchcraft and Fenris, lord of wolves."

The girl put her hands on her hips. "What kind of 'test' do you have in mind?"

Roland winced. "Don't encourage him, Bailey."

Ignoring the wizard, the god said, "Trial by combat, of course. Let us see how you fare against my father's host of fallen heroes."

Roland slapped a hand over his eyes, tilting back his head and groaning.

Baldur snapped his fingers and the holy spirits of the courageous dead appeared around them, summoned from Valhalla. Their forms coalesced out of the wisps of fog, translucent men clad in Dark Age armor, although some were clad only in hide pants or loincloths, and a few wore more modern accoutrements.

All had weapons, and they raised them, letting out war cries that collectively sounded like the howling wind of a gale.

Bailey fell into a fighting stance instantly out of habit. "All right, then," she growled.

Their foes, being ghosts, couldn't be confronted using physical force. Bailey first tried raising a magical shield on both her and Roland's flanks. Transparent sheets of reddish light appeared, and the apparitions, on coming into contact with them, were slowed as though trying to wade through molasses.

That gave Roland enough time to launch an attack.

"Haaaaaa!" He spread his fingers, and multiple bolts of lightning raged toward the new wraiths. They were not huge and powerful, but threatening enough, and the warrior spirits who took them full in the face were frozen in place, crackling with static, before winking out of sight. Returned, perhaps, to the sacred dimension from which they'd been called.

Bailey figured Viking ghosts couldn't be too much different from either the shadow wraiths or the mist demons they'd fought before, both of which were susceptible to fire. She conjured a giant blaze and then sent it rolling toward where her adversaries were thickest, watching with satisfaction as it left only wisps of smoke.

Still, Baldur's army was enormous. The pair fought well, but the numbers they faced never seemed to dwindle.

"Hey!" Roland shouted, "Didn't I just vaporize that asshole a minute ago?"

Bailey was busy pushing back a crowd of berserkers with a wave of concussive force and had no time to examine the asshole in question.

"Shit," the wizard went on. "I did! Goddammit. I just remembered…"

Bailey cringed inwardly. *Uh-oh. Kinda doubt this is going to be good news*, she thought.

Roland's voice remained audible even over the racket of combat, so he might have been amplifying its volume via a spell. "Those who are taken into Odin's hall are blessed by being able to fight endlessly, resurrected each time they're killed. That means that when we toast these guys, they're just popping back to Valhalla. At that point, our shiny friend up there," he gestured toward Baldur, "can summon them right back here."

Bailey suddenly felt cold. For a second, her next attack, a lightning bolt that dissipated the ax-wielding revenant in front of her, almost faltered.

If what the wizard said was true, the battle was unwinnable—not that she intended to go out without a damn good fight.

"Give 'em hell!" she screamed. "We'll make them sick of jumping back and forth till they stage a fuckin' mutiny!"

Roland trapped a few warriors inside a dome of green plasma. "I don't think it works that way, babe."

Bailey watched him for a second. The ghosts he'd just ensorcelled couldn't move and seemed reluctant to just plow into the deadly energy around them. That gave her an idea.

"Well, they can't get cycled back if they're still here," she pointed out.

She summoned air to surge toward the raging host, air from which she'd sucked every iota of heat. The freezing wind washed over them and frost formed around their ectoplasmic bodies, which soon stopped fighting, encased as they were in ice.

"Hah!"

Roland saw what she'd done. "Good idea." He turned toward a column of Vikings advancing toward him with swords and shields and conjured a torrential downpour of liquid nitrogen. The effects were the same as Bailey's freezing wind.

Then, a few of the phantasms emerged from their icy coffins. They moved slowly but were undeterred, much as they'd gradually pushed through the arcane shields moments ago.

"Damn," Bailey panted, cursing her overconfidence. Their foes didn't have material bodies, so they couldn't be converted into immobile solids.

Baldur flourished his arms and even more ghosts appeared around them, as though he'd emptied half of Valhalla to swell the ranks of the undead legion.

There was no way Bailey and Roland could win, and they knew it. It was a battle of attrition they were doomed to lose.

Grimly, trying not to succumb to despair, they backed away, slowing the specters with ice or arcane essence or vaporizing them with fire or lightning.

Soon they had a cluster of trees at their backs, so densely grown that they formed a veritable wall. It might stop, or at least slow, any attempt by the specters to attack them from the rear, but it also meant they were trapped.

Bailey thought of something. "He said he wanted to test us, not kill us."

Roland formed a long sword out of green plasma and swung it at two fighters in front of him, cleaving them in half and reducing their temporary bodies to steam.

"Given how Valhalla seems to operate," he responded, bitter sarcasm in his voice, "it could be that this is Baldur's way of inducting us. In other words, the whole idea is for us to die in combat. Get it?"

She did. Before her, the host of the risen slain swelled like an oncoming tidal wave.

Moments later, still fighting no matter how hopeless, both the wizard and the werewitch found themselves depleted and surrounded. Any move they made would invite the stroke of some arcane weapon, which they somehow knew would be just as deadly as a real one.

But no such blow came. The dead heroes stopped, poised to kill but seeming to wait for something.

Baldur raised a hand over his head. "*Halt,*" he called, his voice echoing across the bogs like an entire marching band's worth of golden trumpets.

Bailey and Roland stood heaving, eyes wide and hair wild and stringy, trying to gear themselves down from the mad rush of combat. The warrior spirits, having neglected to press the attack, now fell back, their swords and spears and axes resting on the damp ground.

The god of light was watching them from his position just up the slope, fingers stroking his beautifully shaped chin. "I see," he stated in a softer but no less melodious voice. "Very interesting."

The young woman wiped sweat from her brow and moved the hand back through her hair, slicking it away from her face. "So, did we pass?" She was worried that the answer would be no since the spirits probably could have killed them if they'd wanted to.

Baldur walked a few paces closer toward them. He looked almost confused by the question. "I discovered much I wanted to know," he replied. "Namely, that you do not pose an immediate threat to the gods."

Roland coughed. "Thanks."

"However," the tall deity went on, "you clearly have the potential. Both of you are stronger than usual for mortal weavers of spells. Also, you fight well together, almost like soldiers who have served side by side in many conflicts."

Bailey nodded. She and the wizard had battled together a hell of a lot of times by now, even if they'd only known each other for maybe two months.

Baldur raised both hands and looked from side to side at the spectral host he'd summoned. "Heroes of old who died bravely in battle, your task here is ended. Return now to Valhalla and Sessrúmnir until you are called upon again."

The sound from before, like a clanging gong of tremendous size, spread across the plain, and the Viking spirits slowly faded like night mist burned away by the sun.

Watching this, the werewitch and the wizard emptied their lungs in relief and relaxed their postures. Both wondered if the incorporeal warriors would have destroyed them or stopped at the moment of truth, as they had a moment ago. For now, nothing suggested that Baldur would threaten them with anything further. The danger had ended.

The god did, however, stride toward them, each footfall ringing an invisible bell and creating a flash of light.

Bailey wondered why no such effects happened when Marcus moved around, but then remembered that he usually traveled in disguise. What she saw before her was Baldur's true form, comparable to the towering wolf-beast Fenris had reverted to when he'd finally revealed his identity.

The deity stopped about ten paces from them. "Tell me," he asked pleasantly but with an enigmatic twist of curiosity on his mildly smiling mouth, "why has Fenris seen fit to train you? What is it about you two that so greatly arouses his interest?"

Bailey seemed confused or annoyed by the question, so Roland figured he'd have to be the one to answer it. He almost made a smartass quip focused on "arouse" but thought better of it. Baldur's oddly pure and naïve personality was such that he probably wouldn't get the joke.

Instead, he figured it wouldn't hurt to cover for her.

"Well," he intoned, "I think Fenris has no serious interest in me. I'm not one of his 'children,' so to speak, so he just figures he might as well help me fine-tune my magic a bit. Probably the same thing with both of us."

Baldur cocked his head to the side. "And yet Bailey is one of his children, so she must be his chief focus. Why?"

Roland hoped Bailey would be smart enough to keep quiet. For his part, he did something he would never have pictured himself doing—giving the silent treatment to a god.

CHAPTER FOUR

Bailey straightened up but otherwise relaxed as the haze of battle receded. She'd found it difficult thus far to come up with any satisfactory answer to Baldur's questions besides the one she'd already given—that Fenris was training her to use her powers responsibly.

As such, she was glad that Roland was stalling the deity with his usual flippant bullshit. Now, he seemed to be reduced to staring the tall, shining man down, and a mortal was guaranteed to lose that sort of contest.

She swallowed some leftover spit and found her voice again.

"Because I have magic," she stated. "It's that simple. It's been a long time since any werewitches were born, just a few male shamans here and there. I guess he wants to make sure I'm trained right, so I know what I'm doing and can help the Were people. I have more power, so he figures I have more responsibility."

She spread her hands, palms toward Baldur, and arched

her eyebrows. It wasn't a shrug; she hoped conveyed something like, *"That's it. What more do you want me to say?"*

Which was, of course, how she felt.

The god tilted his head back to its normal position. "I see. That is most intriguing—that you would be such a rare specimen, and he would desire to see you realize your potential according to such notions of wisdom and justice."

She wasn't sure how to respond to that.

Baldur smiled again in his faint, enigmatic way. "Thank you, mortals, for treating with me. Each of us, the ruling family of Asgard, must take heed of the actions of the others. Now, having tested you, I must go. Farewell."

He gave them a coy nod of the head that was oddly ladylike and then walked back up the slope toward the point where he'd first made his entrance. With a wave of his hand, the massive golden door opened on the realm of crystalline sunlight and the deity vanished into its blazing depths.

The portal slammed shut behind him and disappeared. It left only a faint metallic ringing in the air behind it.

Roland slumped against a tree. "Good lord, I'm glad that's over. *Any* dealings with powerful entities from other planes of existence are potentially hazardous as all fuck. We're more or less humans, and no matter how smart we are, how the *hell* are we supposed to know how a god or a demon or a fairy sprite or an elemental or anything of the sort thinks? You never know where you stand with them."

Bailey stood, hands on her hips, staring at the empty patch of air where the gateway to Asgard had been only a moment ago. Something roiled in her stomach. She was disturbed, but she didn't know why.

She turned to the wizard. "Is that why you seem kinda standoffish with Marcus? Wait, you were like that with him even before we knew who he was."

"Eh, you might say it occurred to me that something about him was a bit…off. Though aside from putting us through all this Spartan crap and never seeming to show up when we need him most, he hasn't done anything I can take issue with, so maybe I'm wrong. But why would Baldur be interested in us?"

The girl was wondering the same thing. "Yeah, it's weird, but like you said, we can't understand their way of thinking. Maybe it's like some, uh, I dunno, upsetting-the-cosmic-balance type of thing."

The wizard stood back up and began strolling casually up the slope. "Could be. Something like that. I'm not an expert on the inner workings of frickin' Valhalla. It makes me curious, though."

Bailey fell into step beside him, slowing her pace once she'd caught up. It occurred to her that she probably knew what Roland was about to say, and she didn't much like it.

"What?" she prompted.

"I'm wondering," he extrapolated, "if there's internal strife going on up there. Office politics, Machiavellian shit, or just plain old family drama. Why is Fenris spending so much time on Earth? What's his standing in the pantheon right now, anyway?"

Bailey frowned. "Well, if we can't understand how the gods think, we sure can't expect to understand all that shit. And the reason Fenris is here is to train us seems pretty damn obvious to me. Or train me, at least. He's taking an interest in us. His 'children,' as he'd say."

"I suppose," the wizard murmured.

They trekked up the gentle slope into a rocky, brambly area. Up ahead was a hillock that looked familiar, probably the one that rose above the Pool of Dark Reflections.

Bailey turned things over in her head, examining them from different sides. "If Baldur is concerned about Fenris, why doesn't he just find him and talk to him? Why ask *us?* Plus, he said something about deciding we weren't a threat to the gods. Maybe the Asgardians have been drinking the same Kool-Aid as those dumbass packs that thought I was gunning for their alphas."

"I don't know," Roland admitted.

They continued toward the hillock. It wasn't the first place they'd seen in the Other—that was an even swampier area, far distant from here—but it was the first place they'd come with Marcus by their side, and where they'd begun their serious training. It seemed like the best place to wait for their teacher.

Neither of them had any desire to descend toward the black pool.

When they were about halfway up the hill, another portal opened at the crest. This one resembled the others they'd see: door-sized and filled with a slow-moving, luminescent purple liquid.

"Well, there he is," Bailey remarked.

"Finally," Roland added.

But the first individual to step out wasn't Marcus. And he was followed by nine others.

Under his breath, Roland grated, "Oh, for fuck's sake!"

The wizard had recognized the new arrivals as Weres. To Bailey, it had been even more obvious. She seldom failed to know her people when she saw them. They were not, however, anyone she'd met before.

The first man to come through, she immediately pegged as the group's leader, and quite possibly the pack alpha. He was a little over six feet tall, with a bulging gut but plenty of muscles to go with it. He had a trimmed beard and a ponytail, both dark brown but streaked with silver. She guessed his age at forty-five or so. He was arguably a bit past his prime, but he still looked formidable.

The others were younger men, ranging from about eighteen to thirty-five, and many of them took after their boss in being bearded and wearing their hair long. All were noticeably dour and dressed in heavy clothes of gray or black.

Roland waved. "Oh, hi. We were just planning on leaving, so you guys can use the Other without us getting in the way. Happy training."

The shadow of a sardonic, crooked smile was briefly visible on the alpha's face. He crossed his burly arms over his broad chest, and behind him, his troops fanned out to block the way to the portal.

"Actually," the man said, "we came for you."

Alarm bells went off in Bailey's head and she stepped forward, preparing to negotiate, explain, and threaten if need be. To her surprise, the troupe seemed totally uninterested in talking.

They shifted in unison, and ten big iron-colored wolf-beasts stood before the pair. Then they attacked.

"*Fuck!*" Bailey exclaimed as the alpha lunged for her She pivoted to the side, speeding up her movement through subtle telekinesis. "No, goddammit! We're just here training! What the hell are you doing?"

Roland snorted. "They're trying to kill us, obviously! I've had it with this shit. Take 'em out. They're your people."

Two wolves jumped at him, their jaws open and trailing drool, and the wizard launched himself twenty feet into the air before floating backward. He kept his hands outstretched to ready a spell, but was hesitant to strike.

Bailey likewise tried to steer clear of the wolves' attacks without hitting back. "Knock this shit off! I'm a shaman's apprentice, and I'm here for training. He'll vouch for me. I don't even know you guys!"

The reply she got was a snapping pair of jaws coming toward her face. She ducked back, seized the wolf around the neck, and hurled him aside, using a bit of magic to send the creature flying farther than he would have otherwise. She also slowed his descent so he didn't break his legs on impact.

"I'm not an enemy!" she shouted, her frustration near the breaking point. If they didn't cease immediately, she'd have to retaliate. "I'm training to be a shaman to werekind under Fenris himself! Haven't you heard? Do you realize what that means?"

A lycanthrope crashed into her from behind. She lost her balance, but by the time she fell to what would have been her hands and knees, she was standing on four legs. Black hair had sprouted all over her body, which was now elongated and lupine, and her eyes glowed red. She growled.

Bailey launched into them, nimbly dodging their

brutish assaults and shouldering pack soldiers aside. She pounded their furred breasts with her paws, sweeping their legs out from under them and wrestling them to the ground by the scruffs of their necks.

But she didn't break limbs or spines or rip out guts or throats.

Roland, watching how his partner in crime fought, picked up on the hint that this wasn't meant to be a battle to the death. He adjusted his tactics accordingly, conjuring magic that would stop, slow, disorient, and possibly injure the Weres, but nothing that was likely to kill them.

A few were charging at him now, so he raised a wall of ice in front of them. It was not so thick that they risked cracking their skulls open on impact, but thick enough that crashing into it, or through it in the case of the biggest one, left them reeling and dizzy or crumpled in shock and lightly bleeding from minor cuts where the ice fractured.

Then he conjured a tornado made of equal parts wind and pure telekinetic arcane force, which scooped up three of the Weres, and spun them in disorienting circles before tossing them into patches of thick, gnarled roots.

With the herd thinned some, Bailey turned her sights on their alpha. She watched the lead wolf closely, her eyes and brain working rapidly to process all pertinent information and timing the way he moved. He was strong and skilled, but not as fast as he likely used to be—and not as fast as she was.

Bailey pounced. Her wolf body, large as it was, passed nimbly under the alpha's claw-swipe and she knocked him over, her jaws clamped around his throat. She growled as loudly as she could.

Within a second, the fighting had stopped. The other werewolves had all turned toward their leader, now helpless and an instant from death if Bailey chose to kill him. Roland too drew back, still alert but not casting spells for the moment.

The girl shifted back into human form. Doing so gave the alpha an opening to strike, and he could have bitten her leg off if he was fast enough. But he didn't, and once she was comfortably back in her usual shape, Bailey put her foot on his throat.

Then she threw up her hands. "Okay, this fight's goddamn over. Now, will everyone please calm the hell down?"

A few low growls emerged, but mostly the wolves looked like they'd lost the will to continue the battle.

"See," Bailey went on, "I just beat your alpha. If I can do that to the strongest of your pack, imagine what I could do to the rest of you. And it looks like Roland was handling you all pretty well, too. None of you are dead. We don't want to kill your asses, even though you earned as much. Now, how about you tell me why the fuck you attacked us?"

Beneath her boot, the alpha shifted back to his human form, now naked. She removed her foot from his neck and allowed him to scooch back and sit up. His pack warriors followed his lead and changed back as well.

Roland let out a half-sigh, half-groan. "Now we're getting somewhere," he quipped. "It's been a long day. Or a long segment of eternity, whatever applies to this bizarre place."

Cautiously, the two factions gathered their shredded

clothing, keeping eyes on each other, and reconfigured their positions so Bailey and Roland soon were on one side of the hilltop and the strangers on the other.

The alpha stood near the front and regarded the pair with heavy-lidded eyes. He was clearly in some pain from the exertions of the battle, combined with how hard Bailey had slammed him into the ground.

"We came here to seek you out on the advice of another pack. Neighbors of ours and friends. Their apprentice shaman told us he had reliable information that you—Bailey—were a threat that had to be dealt with. That you were plotting against our pack and that the shit you've been pulling lately is bringing a lot of attention from those European witches. The same ones who murdered the Junipers' shaman."

For a second, Bailey wanted to double over with grief. Her victory over the Venatori outside of Greenhearth had been rendered bitter by the discovery that they'd killed old Estus.

Then she got angry.

"God-fucking-dammit," she shouted, and the Weres tensed, half-expecting her to start fighting them again. She didn't, though; that wasn't the kind of rage that consumed her now. "How many fucking times do I have to go through this shit? The Junipers were the first pack to come after me because someone gossiped that I was gunning for their alpha. You'd think that if people heard about what happened to their shaman, they'd also have frickin' heard that I made peace with them and they agreed that the rumors were a crock of shit."

The alpha across from her looked almost embarrassed.

"And then," she went on, "the Eastmoors came after me, and one got himself killed, even though I sure as shit didn't want it that way. Them too—they'd heard this crap about me wanting to take over the whole damn Pacific Northwest. Who the hell is spreading this shit? Dan Oberlin's friends? If that's the case, why is anyone listening to a bunch of scumbags who were kidnapping Were girls right out of their own towns? For fuck's sake!"

Roland put a hand on her shoulder. Feeling it there, she started to calm down and slowed her breathing deliberately, deciding she'd ranted enough. They both waited for the mysterious pack to respond.

The leader cast his eyes to the side for a second, then inhaled and puffed himself up. Bailey grasped somehow that he was contrite. Ashamed, even, although he had to save face in front of his men. She'd be willing to meet him halfway as long as he tried to be reasonable.

"Let us introduce ourselves," he said. "My name is Alfred Warner, and we're the Whitcomb Creek Pack. West side of the Cascades between Salem and Eugene. We were acting on what we thought was accurate information in the interest of our pack like anyone would. It wasn't personal. And we appreciate that you didn't try to kill any of us."

His words, she saw, had the effect of calming some of his followers, who looked like they still had half a mind to try ripping her head off.

She nodded and crossed her arms. "Okay. Fair enough. But who gave you that information, which obviously *wasn't* accurate? Like I said, this is the third time someone's tried to take me out, based on slander. All I'm trying to do is learn to handle my powers and become a decent shaman. No bullshit."

Alfred frowned. "I'm sorry, but I can't tell you that. Only so much we can share without breaking the bonds of friendship we have. Different packs, different people. You know how it is. Different shamans we've got mutual loyalty to. We're not from your town, and we don't owe you any counter-information that might lead to reprisals against our cousins."

He said that in a somber, borderline-apologetic way, softening the impact of his words, although she suspected he wouldn't budge if she pressed him on it.

Before she could respond, he continued. "But I will say I no longer believe what I'd heard. You're tough and have an attitude, but your heart seems to be in the right place. You refrained from killing any of us, even when you probably could have, and now here we are, talking things out. That tells me you're honest about trying to be a good shaman. You care about the welfare of wolves in general, not just your pack, your town, or your base of knowledge."

Roland fidgeted, confused by the man's direct way of speaking. On some level, he still didn't understand the rules of werewolf society.

Alfred smiled. "So, if you ever swing by our neck of the woods, I owe you a drink."

He turned around and motioned for the younger men to follow him. They all trudged toward the portal they'd come through, which still stood open.

"See ya," one of the bucks called as though they were old friends. Then the ten of them filed through the gateway. Seconds later, it vanished.

Roland shook his head slowly. "Well, that was an adventure. I think. What just happened?"

Bailey scowled. "Dumbass. You heard him. Some dickhead lied to them, so here they came. At least they were smart enough to believe me once I had the opportunity to talk to them. End of story, *aside* from the matter of who this guy is who sent them after me."

"Yeah," the wizard agreed. "That part bothers me. Their neighbor pack's apprentice shaman? And these are people you don't even know?"

The girl stared into the distance. "It doesn't make any sense, but we've got to figure it out. And I know just the man to ask—if he ever shows back up."

CHAPTER FIVE

Fortunately, it wasn't much longer when Marcus, at long last, reappeared.

He didn't step out of a portal; rather, he emerged from the nearby forest and then walked, slowly and casually, up the hillock toward them. Whatever business he'd been on, it must have been something within the Other, rather than back on Earth.

"You know," Roland commented to Bailey, although he was sure Marcus could hear him, "the other ones tend to be a little more dramatic with their entrances."

Bailey flicked his ear. "Yeah, and also more likely to 'test' us with random acts of combat twenty seconds after they show up. At least Marcus had the decency to ask if we wanted his help first."

The tall man, still wearing his bulky hooded coat, crested the rise and stood before them. "What are you talking about?"

Roland laughed and rubbed his forehead. "Hoo, boy. Have we got a story for you! Two of them, in fact."

Marcus looked at Bailey. "Tell me."

The delayed emotional impact of all that had transpired hit the girl all at once, and as soon as she opened her mouth, the words rushed out. "Yeah, we'll tell you, and then we've got a shit-ton of questions for you as well. *Goddamn*, Marcus, how does this stuff even keep happening? And where the heck were you? Don't leave us alone in here again! Weres, witches, and now even gods are all coming after us."

"Yup!" Roland chirped, a wild gleam in his eye. "*Gods*. Ha-ha. Crazy, right? Armies of ghosts. The divine sort, not the native rabble. Things just keep getting more interesting."

The shaman held up his hands, blinking within his hood. "Slow down. I don't understand what you're talking about. You're safe now, so just take a deep breath and start from the beginning. I can't help you if you don't explain things clearly."

Somehow, the man's demeanor helped them calm down. Even despite their confusion and suspicions, the simple fact that he was willing to listen while they talked it out made it easier to discuss.

They told him how they'd reconvened by the campfire, only to encounter Baldur shortly after they'd left. How the god wanted to know what they were doing and saw fit to test them in battle against a host of warrior spirits. Hearing this, Marcus' face was grave, but he only nodded and waited for them to go on.

They then described how they had been attacked by the Whitcomb Creek Pack, in much the same fashion as the Junipers and Eastmoors had come after them previously.

They relayed how disturbed they were that this mysterious apprentice shaman was spreading rumors that they needed to be taken out.

Through it all, Bailey was mostly curious and hurt by the implication that she was doing something bad, despite her just wanting to grow into her responsibilities and stand up for her people.

Roland, on the other hand, seemed borderline paranoid about the entire situation. He also didn't miss the opportunity to wonder why Baldur was so curious about the doings of his Asgardian kin.

Fenris, wearing his imposing yet unremarkable human form, gave a final nod as they concluded their story. "I see," he rumbled.

"Good," Roland said curtly.

Bailey just gazed at her teacher. First of all, she had to know about Baldur and what it meant for their relationship as master and student.

Marcus seemed to sense that and addressed it immediately. "First, I understand your concern about my cousin's visit. It stems from a long and complicated history of what you might call 'family business.' There's almost no way for me to explain it to mortals, but I can reassure you it won't happen again. Freya and Baldur have both conducted their tests, and the results have been in your favor."

"Okay," Bailey replied, although his words didn't make her feel better. "It worried me because it almost sounded like he, Baldur, thought you were doing something wrong."

Marcus shook his head, frowning into the shadows. "I have never been on very good terms with my family, thanks to my connection with werewolves. The Norsemen of old fought them at times, regarding them as sources of strife and chaos, and people they banished from their societies were treated as 'lone wolves' whom anyone might slay. Taking the Were people as my children has made me the…black sheep, you might say, in Asgard."

A smile of sardonic, almost vicious amusement spread across his face at that.

"Pardon me," he added. "The irony of it! The god of wolves, comparing himself to a sheep."

"Oh, ha," Bailey commented. "Right, right. I guess that clarifies things somewhat, but I still feel like we're in more danger than we already were."

The shaman waved a hand. "I will take care of it. It's not your concern anymore. My family will, if necessary, hear me out and learn to leave us to our own affairs."

Roland piped up. "What about the pack that jumped us? Bailey said she's never even met those guys. Why would they still be gunning for her when we already demonstrated to those previous groups that Bailey *isn't* trying to take over their leadership?"

Marcus gave a shrug of his wide shoulders. "It's hard to say, but the overall situation concerned me from the beginning. Revealing yourself and your powers would naturally draw attention. And now that I've revealed myself? Well, that has lent you legitimacy, but in other ways, it might have made it worse. The lofty invariably attract the jealous and the envious."

The wizard's eyes rolled. Not in sarcastic skepticism, Bailey noticed, but in thoughtfulness. What Marcus had just said was a near-perfect description of what Roland had gone through as a kid.

The shaman went on. "Someone ambitious, who perhaps feels threatened by your rise—this other shaman's apprentice, perhaps—might have decided that he can make a name for himself by targeting you. Maybe he thinks that with you out of the way, Bailey, he can take your place, and have the honor of training under me. Or he might legitimately believe the paranoid gossip that you plan to depose all other shamans and alphas, despite what's happened recently."

Bailey nodded. "That makes sense. Oh, also, the Whitcomb alpha Alfred mentioned something about them worrying that I'm attracting the attention of the Venatori." Her face fell. "I guess he was right about that, but the cat's out of the bag. I never meant to let it out, and I don't know how to put it back in."

Marcus laid a hand on her shoulder, and some of her stress melted away. "I will do more to shield you and hide you while you're in the Other. In that much at least, I admit fault. Otherwise, don't trouble yourself with these things."

"So," Roland asked, "what should we do?"

The god of wolves smiled grimly. "Keep training."

Thirteen women stood on a low ridge lined with mossy pine trees and looked down on the little settlement. They made no effort to hide since they knew they were well-concealed.

"Cute," remarked Madame MacLachlan as she surveyed the premises.

It was a werewolf community disguised as a mobile

home village in the middle of the rustic area near the Capitol State Forest, south of Washington's capital of Olympia. The strawberry-blonde witch had to admit it was clever. By concentrating all their people in the area within a single trailer park, the Were pack was able to hide in plain sight, separate from nearby human towns, without needing many people who could be trusted to maintain silence.

Of course, it was also a cheap, low-class place, exactly what she would expect of American lycanthropes.

One of the apprentice-level witches she'd brought turned to her. "When do we strike, Madame?"

MacLachlan didn't look at her. "In a minute or two. Just need to check for traffic."

She sent her mind out to scry for oncoming cars who might witness what was about to happen. There didn't seem to be any since the trailer park was located on a back road that few people would have cause to take unless they lived there.

Another young sorceress fidgeted. "Just give the word, Madame. We are ready."

MacLachlan ignored her. It was mildly annoying to have the grunts pressuring her, but at least it meant they were enthusiastic.

She'd picked them out of the Venatori's lower ranks on the basis of obedience, motivation, and destructive skill. Any who'd expressed hesitation, she passed over and chose someone else instead. All twelve of them *wanted* to be here.

MacLachlan didn't particularly, but she wasn't about to disobey the Grandmistress. At least, not in the grand scheme of things. She had rather different ideas than

Madames Gregorovia and Dorleac seemed to about how the situation should be handled. MacLachlan felt now was the time to send a message.

They'd used a powerful but convenient teleportation spell to send themselves to a small coastal town in British Columbia, a location the Venatori had used before when they had business in the region, then stowed away on a cargo ship bound for Tacoma, near Seattle. From there, it was a simple matter to slip past the authorities and secure transportation that would take them south into Oregon.

In fact, since they'd made such good time, MacLachlan saw no reason why they *shouldn't* make a few stops along the way. They could use a nice training exercise for the new recruits.

MacLachlan pointed at the trailer park and ordered, her tone casually amused, "Attack."

The young witches dashed forward, spreading out in a crescent formation, a skirmish line that would quickly wrap around the settlement and then engulf it. Once they were beyond the danger of friendly fire, they started tossing lightning bolts at the metal siding of the mobile homes.

MacLachlan watched from a hundred meters back, encasing the little community in a soundproof magical dome as small thunderclaps rang out. The first of the frightened werewolves burst out of their homes, confused and panicked. Many had half-shifted into their hideous lupine forms, some with burnt fur from the havoc the electrical blasts had wrought.

The primitive beasts attempted to fight back, and MacLachlan supposed it qualified as a brave attempt. But even with the Weres' superior numbers, it was a massacre. The Venatori had the element of surprise, combined with powerful magic that far exceeded mere shapeshifting. It was an unfortunate but necessary exercise.

There was one casualty. The apprentice who'd asked when they were going to attack had taken a nasty bite on the leg and now writhed and moaned in pain on the ground. Healing the wound wouldn't be too difficult.

A single survivor slipped past the twelve—a middle-aged woman, still in human form, her eyes rolling wildly as she stumbled across the sward toward MacLachlan. She didn't even see the Venatori woman.

The sorceress stepped forward. "Can't allow that, I'm afraid." She gestured at the woman, who folded to the ground and didn't move again.

The leader strode up to her followers. "Fine work," she said, momentarily ignoring the screams of the injured young witch. "Just like I said—dead easy. They didn't even know what hit them, but the rest of them will know that they cannot strike at us and fail to pay the price."

The witches nodded grimly. A couple of them, who hadn't seen real violence before, looked a bit sick, but they'd get over it. It was all for the cause, after all.

"And," MacLachlan added, holding up a finger, "we're thinning out their ranks. Fewer of the bastards to deal with later when the shite hits the fan."

She reflected with grim amusement on Madame Gregorovia's nonsensical statement about avoiding an escalation of hostilities. Might as well hit hard and hit *first*, and win the war before they had a chance to lose it.

The new girl, the one who'd said, "Just give the word," smirked. Her name was Rhona if MacLachlan recalled.

"Is this the best werewolves can do?" she mused.

MacLachlan glared at her. "Don't get overconfident. This was just a warm-up for those of you who don't have much experience. Our main target is Bailey Nordin, who's a far cry from these oafs. She killed at least two of ours, and they were witches of decent caliber. That's the whole reason we're here."

The younger women nodded and saluted, even Rhona.

"And," their leader went on, "she's no ordinary lycanthrope. She's a werewitch, a rare combination with access to magic on par with our own, even if she's too green and stupid to use it with the same level of finesse that we do. But the plot thickens…"

Most of them had already been briefed on the situation, but a few were last-minute replacements. It would benefit them all to hear a clear assessment as a group and help forge the coven-mind toward their ultimate goal.

"She's got a male witch with her, probably her lover, who's also quite powerful. For a man, anyway. He might be training her in the proper use of the arcane. Plus, there's this mysterious shaman she's made contact with. I have no doubt that we will win in the end, but we must take this chore seriously. Those of you who *don't,* risk ending up like Madame Lavonne."

That was clear enough. By handing them an easy victory, she had allowed them to apply their skills in a "real" situation, but now it was important to ensure that they didn't get cocky.

She didn't want to terrify them, though, so she

refrained from mentioning that the so-called shaman might be a god. Possibly.

"Come, then," MacLachlan ordered. "Burn all the houses. The authorities will assume someone left their coffee pot plugged in for too long or something, but the conspicuous pile of bodies will make people nervous all the same. Just what we want. And at our next stop, we'll give the Weres a little advance warning before we eliminate them. You'll have the opportunity to confront their kind in something more like a fair fight."

The witches went about their task, and soon the entire trailer park was blazing. There was no way to hide a conflagration of that size, and sirens approached.

As the Venatori took their leave, MacLachlan reflected on how lopsided the whole conflict was likely to be. Her group was only the advance force, the shock troops. Madame Gregorovia had promised to send reinforcements soon.

Once the Scotswoman informed her of how things had "accidentally" gotten out of control, the council would have no choice but to send even more. Soon MacLachlan would lead half the Order's army to victory.

A lone man stood and watched the fires grow. He noted the direction the thirteen women went—southeast, of course—but his attention was mainly focused on the carnage they'd left behind and the small bleeping device in his hands.

"Damn," Agent Townsend muttered. "That's about all there is to say, isn't it? Just…*damn*."

He'd gotten there too late to intervene in any meaningful way. Besides, he'd had no idea they'd planned to do this. Even by the Venatori's standards, what had just happened was beyond the pale.

He could have grabbed a gun, leapt in, and played the hero. He might have been able to toast one or two of them before they reduced him to a splotch on the ground—just like the late Agent Spall.

The witches would move on with their mission anyway, and the whole trailer park would still be dead and in flames. Then there wouldn't be anyone to report on their movements or coordinate an effort to stop them.

Townsend took a deep breath. Watching the Weres get slaughtered hadn't been fun. However, he knew that, under the circumstances, he'd done the right thing by keeping himself alive to fight another day.

The gadget he held before him sort of resembled an old Game Boy Color from the 90s. He remembered when the damn things had first come out. Of course, the Agency device bore no resemblance to a Game Boy in function, only in form.

Specifically, it noted concentrations of magic in carbon-based material. Arcane expulsions tended to react with blood, hence the many magical traditions, especially the blacker sort, that employed blood as the main component of their rituals. There were significant concentrations of witchcraft in the stains that now littered the destroyed trailer park, and he'd managed to document most of them before the whole place went up in flames.

Having documented that magic-users were responsible for the massacre, he'd soon be able to bring the full force of the Agency—with the strength of the entire U.S. government to back it up—to bear on those responsible.

"Fuck," he muttered. "This would be easier if I wasn't alone. I'm not used to this shit, Spall. Didn't you consider that? Asshole."

Saying that out loud, if only under his breath, made it feel like someone had just kicked him in the stomach, but once it passed, he felt a little better. The device in his hands finished its beeping as the sirens grew louder, then stopped. The fire department was here.

Townsend ran a hand through his thinning hair and stood up, preparing to speak to the local authorities and take command of the situation. It would be best if he waited in the shadows and arrived on the scene after the firefighters and cops had a chance to "control" the situation.

Of course, this time, he'd have to do one hundred percent of the talking.

"Don't worry, Spall," he whispered. "You might have been a dumbass at the end, getting yourself killed, but your heart was in the right fuckin' place. At least you got two of them. I'll get the rest. Send 'em straight to hell so you can finish dealing with them."

He was looking forward to it.

"Nah," he chided himself. "Just a duty that has to be done. A categorical imperative. For every action, there is an equal and opposite reaction."

In the war to come, it was possible other agents would end up dead, too. But then, the Agency had never sought this. They weren't the ones who'd started it. *All* the blood-shed, starting two weeks ago, was the Venatori's fault.

Townsend would make damn sure that *all* of it got pinned directly to their asses.

As the fire truck pulled up, he breathed in and out a few times, clearing his headspace in preparation for being an emotionless professional when he spoke to the locals. Professionalism was important. Especially when he had to admit that the whole goddamn thing was now *personal*.

Nicolas Jezak, apprentice to shaman Fred Grotowski of the Shashka Pack, stood staring with eyes that were wide but somehow blank and hollow with the horror of what he was seeing. A faint tremor of anger went through the ropey muscles of his lean frame.

His teacher didn't have time to instruct him as often as he'd like, so the training was going slowly. As such, Nick had plenty of time to do other things on the side, such as accompany another shaman, Marcus, on a little sightseeing tour.

The older man extended a hand toward the smoldering crime scene. "You see?" he said. "This is the kind of thing that's already begun to happen, and I'm afraid it's going to keep getting worse until things change in a major and important way."

Nick's voice was almost raspy as he swallowed the lump in his throat and asked, "What happened? In the name of fucking Fenris, how did this happen?"

The shaman had taken him through a shortcut in the

Other to view the scene unfolding south of Olympia, Washington. The two of them crouched inconspicuously in the forest shadows near what used to be a peaceful little trailer park.

Three of four entire square acres had been reduced to charcoal. The inky-black smoke was still rising in places, even after the fire department had drenched the whole place with water. Now cops and paramedics milled about.

They were loading many, many body bags onto stretchers. Putting them in the back of a cargo truck, even.

Marcus sighed. "I might be able to show the final moments of some who died here, a holographic projection of sorts. It would shed light on the nature of the tragedy. But if we do that, I don't think we're going to like what we see."

Nick clenched and unclenched his bony fists. "I *already* don't like it. Show me."

"As you wish," replied Marcus, sadness in his voice.

He concentrated, recited a brief chant, and spread his hands before the awful scene. That darkness was falling now somehow made it worse since it obscured the details and left too much to the imagination.

A disc of light, purplish-silver in hue, spread on the ground before them like a perfectly circular pool of water. Within it, a movie of the past played out.

They both watched in disgust as screaming, snarling, terrified werewolves piled out of burning mobile homes, their bodies distorted by half-finished shifting, as sometimes happened when a Were was in a bad state of mind. Magical lightning and fire flashed all around. Men, women, and children collapsed in heaps. In the end, fire consumed everything.

Nick looked away, waving his hand, and Marcus snapped his fingers to dismiss the scrying. The images vanished and left only shadows behind. Somehow, the scry had been unable to reveal who had perpetrated it. They only saw the victims, probably because they were the ones whose psychic residues were most strongly tied to the location.

The shaman watched, unspeaking, as the younger man doubled over, holding his breath as he struggled not to vomit. After about two minutes, he stood back up, crossing his tattooed bare arms over his chest.

"Whoever did this," he stated, "is going to pay."

Marcus nodded. "It's tragic that it's come to this. We have to act before similar tragedies befall other Weres all over the Pacific Northwest. It won't be easy, though. Whoever did this, it was clearly someone with a great deal of magical power."

"I can see that," Nick snapped. "It would be helpful if we saw who the fuck it was, but I think I can narrow it down to one or two likely possibilities."

The shaman said nothing.

Nicholas Jezak, as near as Marcus could tell, was a channeler of above-average ability. His powers weren't extraordinary, but they were enough to pose a legitimate threat to most opponents. Rather than raw power, the apprentice's chief assets were his connections and his persuasive ability, possibly the sign that he was gifted in psychic magic above all else. It was a useful skill for someone who already had a surplus of friends.

He was also impatient with the glacial progress of his training and hungry for an opportunity to advance himself more quickly.

Knowing this, Marcus wasn't surprised in the slightest when Nick asked the next question.

The younger man stared into the shaman's eyes, his jaw trembling with the tension of the muscles along it. "Where is she?"

CHAPTER SIX

"I should have known," Roland grumbled, "that the son of a bitch would send us back *here*. Sorry. Am I allowed to call a god a 'son of a bitch?' I don't think he's around to hear, but you never know with supernatural beings who are multiple orders of magnitude above us on the scale of…everything."

They sat in the muddy sand just past the edge of the Pool of Dark Reflections, their least favorite place in the Other. However, Bailey had to admit the black lake had been instrumental in the progress of both of them so far.

"Yeah, yeah," she shot back, giving Roland a disapproving glare. "Fenris understands mortals way better than the other gods do, it seems like. He might cut you some slack for saying that shit, knowing how tired and stressed out we both are. But I wouldn't try it to his face."

The wizard flexed his hands. "Oh, I wouldn't *dream* of doing such a thing."

Bailey tried not to shudder. "Don't mention dreams

right now. We've had enough of the bad kind, thanks to this place."

Not only had they seen Aida Nassirian, one of Roland's "admirers" and the right-hand woman of Shannon DiGrezza, dragged into the pool to her death by the realm's mist-demons, but the mysterious power of the waters had induced highly unpleasant visions in both of them. It seemed to force people to confront their worst fears.

Fortunately, the task Marcus had set for them didn't involve succumbing to any more waking nightmares. The opposite, in fact. He'd told them to gently channel magic toward themselves through the pool, then try to *resist* the onset of the visions.

It was some kind of defense against psionic attacks, Bailey suspected. The Venatori had tried to overwhelm them previously with waves of terror and despair, so it made sense to know how to protect themselves.

"Well," Roland commented, "we probably ought to get back to it. I'll be the first to confess that this nonsense isn't easy. Essentially, he's having us deliberately induce an altered state of consciousness, which makes it harder to cast spells, then use rational magic to push back or something like that. Shit."

Bailey shrugged. "It's for a good reason. The more we know how to do, the harder it will be for the witches to kill us. Or in your case, enslave you and use you as a sperm donor."

Roland stretched his legs. "It's nice to have a woman to talk to about these things. Every time I mention that particular situation to another man, they produce the same old jokes about how much they'd like to be 'threatened' with the 'doom' I'm trying to get the fuck away from. Doesn't it occur to them that being reduced to a vending machine would get old pretty fast?"

The girl shook her head. "Men!"

They languished without speaking for a bit, neither wanting to provoke the dreaded pool again but having no idea of what else they might do if they rebelled against Marcus' instructions.

It had occurred to both of them, though. Bailey was almost ashamed of her feelings, but she couldn't deny them, either. She was frustrated by the slow, tedious, tortuous path of her training. The seemingly endless strain and repetition, and the lack of clear answers as to why they did what they did.

Marcus' method of instruction was like making them fight their way through fog with blindfolds and earplugs in the hope that it would develop their tactile reflexes, not caring what it did to the quality of their hand-eye or ear-eye coordination. Or their planning and strategic skills.

Just as they were about to get up, something out in the pool began to bubble.

"What the hell?" Roland pointed at it. "That looks bad. What do you say we get the fuck out of here?"

Bailey stared. The black liquid, too dark and viscous to be water, was rising fountain-like around a mass—no, a *figure*—emerging from the depths of the lake.

The werewitch and the wizard jumped to their feet, spines going cold. They knew they ought to just run, but they were weirdly fascinated. Some part of them wanted to know what was boiling its way out.

"Shit!" Bailey exclaimed. "The goddamn pool is

spawning another vision, and this time we didn't notice it was happening. We're not *that* tired yet, are we? How long have we been in here?"

Roland swallowed and took a couple of steps back, dragging on the girl's arm to encourage her to do the same.

"We're *not* that tired," he answered her, "and this isn't a vision. It's real. Something is coming out of the water, and it's guaranteed not to be anything good."

That was just what she was afraid of.

All at once, the thing stood up. The water out there looked deep, yet what emerged was a humanoid shape that towered far enough above the surface that it only appeared to come up to its knees. It looked like a giant plant or a fungus or a mass of algae the same obsidian color as the water, rotten, dripping, and hideous. It had long wet black hair and limbs composed of vines and tendrils wound tightly around decaying chunks of flesh and bone.

Roland made a strangled hissing sound. "Oh, my fucking god!"

The creature was looking at them with wide dark eyes that were somehow familiar. It opened its mouth and out poured a torrent of bile and seaweed-like sludge before it found its voice.

Though the thing now stood in the open air, the sound that emerged from its pond-scum-lined throat resembled something shouted underwater, combined with a bizarre sibilance that reminded Bailey of the wind rushing through a field of grass.

"*You!*" it jeered. "You did this. You two did this to me! It's all your fault. Look at me! *Look at me!*"

Bailey snapped her eyes toward Roland, trying to gauge

his reaction. He had shut his eyelids and was quaking in place like a kid having a nightmare.

"Roland," she urged, shaking him by the shoulder. "Is it…"

"Yes," he stated, his voice low and ragged. "It's fucking Aida."

Staring at the abomination, Bailey was forced to accept the truth. The young woman who'd been dragged into the accursed lake not long ago hadn't died but had somehow mutated into one of the Other's myriad demons.

Horribly, her tall and ample-bosomed figure and well-chiseled facial features were still vaguely recognizable, despite how much of her body had been consumed or replaced by alien plant life. Enough of her former beauty remained for them to be nauseated by how badly it had been ruined.

"I," the Aida-thing went on with a sloshy groan, "am now part of this place. I thought I died, but I didn't. I stayed alive, even as I was turned into fertilizer for the things that grow at the bottom of this lake. Now I belong to it, and the Other belongs to me. I am a manifestation of the cursed bog, the endless swamps here that hunger for mortal flesh and blood and souls. And I can't think of *anyone* who deserves that fate more than you. Come, join me!"

Bailey blinked, suddenly spurred to action. "*Hell, no.* Roland, let's ditch her."

"Good idea," he agreed. They turned and sprinted up the slope, fighting the steep terrain and the pull of gravity to get out of sight of the awful pond.

Aida's voice gurgled after them. "No! Come back! You *will* fucking pay! I can't even *die!* I'm in hell!"

In front of them, the weeds and mosses and roots rose up like a mass of charmed snakes emerging from an Indian fakir's basket, slithering over to block their path, then moving in for the kill.

Bailey raised a hand and sucked the heat out of the mass of plant matter, paralyzing it with cold and causing some of the vines to break off. Then she spun, the heat she'd stolen forming a fireball in front of her hand, and threw it straight at Aida.

"You tried to kill me with one of these," Bailey reminded her. "Now we'll see about the whole 'not dying' thing."

The mass of flames struck the swamp creature square in the chest. Half the fire was extinguished at once by the dampness of Aida's body and the residual bubbling vapors of the lake, but the other half seemed to engulf her. She screamed, but only for a couple of seconds. Then the blaze winked out, and only steam rose where it had burned.

Bailey stared. "Fucking hell!"

Part of Aida's new body had been destroyed by the blast, but almost sentient black water was rising to cover the damage. The botanical tendrils and blobs of pond moss were regenerating at an unnaturally fast rate.

"So," Roland observed, his face skewed with that half-crazed look he got when he could barely believe what he was seeing, "she's a kudzu plant now, basically. Let's try some weed-killer."

He swept his arms toward the mutated witch and a cloud of toxic vapor condensed into a sheet of yellowish rain that poured down on their foe, raising puffs of smoke where it struck.

"So, yeah, Aida," Roland called. "I know a thing or two about the chemical composition of herbicides. Unlike *other* people, I paid attention in science class instead of texting my friends about whose makeup looked like shit that day."

Aida shrieked, the noise unnervingly inhuman, and she half-melted, half-withered, sinking partway back into the boggy pool. Again the black liquid came to her rescue, neutralizing the attack and re-growing her ravaged body.

Then, her still-mostly-human eyes flashing with hate, Aida struck back.

Vines sprouted from the earth around Bailey's and Roland's ankles, lashing them into place, while a foaming column of black liquid rose from the lake and splashed uphill toward them.

"Dammit," Bailey growled, weakening the vines with a wave of heat and then tearing them apart. Roland did likewise, and the two of them dove in opposite directions to avoid the crashing wave of enchanted liquid.

It reached for them with dark dripping tentacles, then flowed back downhill, compelled somehow to return to the pool. Aida gave a strangled cry of frustrated rage.

Roland caught Bailey's eye. "This isn't working. We need to get her away from the pool so she can't regenerate."

"Yeah," the girl replied, "or kill her outright by using more firepower."

They scrambled the rest of the way up the slope and climbed over the ridge onto the hillock.

"Or both," Roland suggested. "That way, we can kill her

make sure she doesn't regenerate, and keep blasting the ashes until they're reduced to subatomic particles."

Behind them, they could hear the sloshing sound of something moving through the pond in the direction they'd fled.

"Yeah," quipped Bailey, "let's go with Option Number Three."

The pair scrambled over the weedy expanse of the hill-top, reasoning that if nothing else, they could probably outdistance their adversary with ease. The wet, shuffling noises were moving no faster than a brisk trot. Aida had probably lost the ability to run.

"No!" her distorted voice screamed again. "You *won't* get away! You *deserve* this!"

Roland tripped. "Shit!" he gasped, pitching forward, his arms flailing before they extended to brace himself and save his face from crashing into the ground.

Bailey saw with mounting revulsion that grasping weeds had encircled the wizard's feet and ankles and shins. She jumped into the air, but her left foot, lower than the right, succumbed to the grip of a similar mass of vines. She stumbled and half-rolled on her side in the writhing foliage.

Regaining her bearings as the sentient plants flowed up her legs, she saw that Roland was using careful blasts of intense cold to destroy the tentacle-like weeds and free himself. She quickly fashioned a crude, glowing blade of arcane plasma and used it to slash the tendrils holding her.

The two sprang to their feet at the same time and bolted.

Ahead of them, a black tree bent over, its branches reaching toward their faces.

Roland had paused to look behind them, and Bailey left him to the task while she summoned lightning to strike the suddenly-hostile tree. Thunder split the air and the dark wood fell asunder, halfway reduced to charcoal.

The wizard groaned. "I don't think we can outrun her. She has too much control over the landscape. At least we got her away from the pond."

The werewitch turned back. "Fight it out, then."

As a wet, mossy head crested the ridge, arm-thick vines and roots sprang from the earth around them, rapidly forming a net, then a dome closing in on them from all directions. Huge spines like lances grew inward, aiming toward their flesh.

"So," Bailey asked, "fire or ice? I'm fine with either."

Roland contemplated the question for a second or two before answering, "Fire. It kills things, guaranteed, whereas some creatures are merely sent into suspended animation or hibernation by being frozen."

Bailey shrugged. "Okay."

In unison, they turned and stood back to back, facing toward the encroaching dome of deadly plants. They extended their arms, channeled or generated heat, and unleashed hell.

Wide swathes of the vines burst into flames. Bailey focused on generating more heat, causing the fire to change color from yellow to green to blue and reducing most of the thorn wall in front of her to a pile of bleached white ash.

Roland, meanwhile, strategically hurled exploding fireballs at the parts of the lattice that directly threatened him, blasting the giant spikes before detonating the wall's foundation. It tottered, and he gave it a telekinetic push so that it fell over and away from him, burnt to cinders.

With the constricting dome obliterated, Aida was revealed to be about two hundred feet away, still shambling slowly toward them. Writhing vines and shuddering waves of moss expanded from her, and she leaked black fluid onto the ground.

Bailey still had control of her wall of fire. She moved it around, finishing off the last of the thorny lattice, then pushed it toward the swamp witch, raising the flames higher to block the deadly spores that now shot at them from the mouths of carnivorous plants. Aida had animated more hybrid creatures from the hill, but she was clearly faltering.

Roland willed a bolt of lightning to fall upon the witch from the sky, paralyzing her and kicking up a great cloud of steam. Then, as Bailey lowered her mass of fire and kept it advancing toward their foe, the wizard tossed a few more exploding fireballs her way.

Aida screamed as she was engulfed in a blaze of heat and smoke and plasma. The few plants she still had control of wilted, even the ones outside the reach of the flames. Her bodily form was breaking down; she was dying.

"Damn you!" her inhuman voice wailed. "I'll be back. The bog will remember!"

The wizard extended both hands in front of him like a character in a fighting game. "Remember this," he said. A raging, almost nuclear fireball, blue-white with intense heat, appeared between his palms, and he cast it at what remained of the witch's chest.

The blast sent a tremor through the ground and gave off so much heat that Bailey and Roland staggered back from it, shielding their faces. When the worst was over, they saw only a pitiful heap of ashes in the center of a blackened circle of ground.

Bailey glanced at the wizard while both caught their breath. He looked as tired as she felt.

"Wanna take a break?" she suggested.

Time had again passed, but not too much. There was still no sign of Marcus, and Roland was having none of it.

"Fuck this shit," he snapped all of a sudden and stood up from the cozy position they'd settled into. "I am completely sick by this goddamn point of waiting for a god to come rescue me from this place. I'm a good wizard. No, a fantastic wizard. I'm opening a portal, and we're going home."

Bailey blinked, then smiled. "Yeah, I'll second that. This is getting old. I could use some damn dinner, even if our stomachs don't work the same way here."

She hoisted herself to her feet. "And if anyone can figure out how to get back through the veil between worlds or whatever it is, it's you."

He beamed with pride. "But of course. I've been watching how our divine friend does it and taking mental notes. He showed me a thing or two as well. I was able to widen that portal the Venatori were using during the battle on the hillside. Granted, opening the doorway seems to be the hard part. Different mindset and skillset from what I'm used to with tricks or combat."

"Tell me," Bailey asked. "I'm curious."

He explained, acknowledging her pointers and questions as he went, that it seemed to be a matter of feeling the arcane makeup of the realm in which they found themselves, then visualizing their destination before finally parting the fabric of reality at that very point. It made sense to her in a general way, although she knew it would prove easier said than done.

Roland inhaled and flexed his hands. "Okay, then. Let's see how this goes."

For several minutes he meditated, concentrated, and hummed faintly under his breath. Then he extended his hands slowly and deliberately before clapping them together and parting them to each side.

The air tore open, disclosing a shimmering mass of purplish liquid. The portal was thin and faint, more of a weak gash between worlds than a proper gateway.

The wizard's brow furrowed, and a bead of sweat rolled down his cheek as he tried to seize the door and force it open wider. For a second, it seemed he'd succeeded—the purple mass broadened near its middle. But then the top and bottom sections collapsed in on themselves, and the whole thing folded inward and faded.

"Shit!" Roland exclaimed. "I lost it. It requires you to focus on multiple things at once in a way I'm not used to. I got close enough, though, that I can probably do it in a couple more tries."

Bailey scratched her chin. "I'll try. Wouldn't hurt to

have two people on the job, after all."

The wizard shrugged. "Sure, why not? Go for it."

The werewitch drew a breath, closed her eyes, and did what Roland had described: feeling the nature of the Other and pulling up images of the point in Greenhearth she wanted to return to. She visualized the patch of forest near Marcus' hut in the foothills just outside town.

She reached out and tore through.

A portal appeared, larger than Roland's but jagged and unstable. The purple liquid surface resembled a lake during a windstorm. For a moment, she almost lost control of it, but then, remembering all she'd learned, she stabilized the edges and flattened the surface. The result was less a neat doorway than the mouth of a cave or tunnel, but it held.

Roland coughed. "Well, then."

Bailey could hardly believe it. She grinned, then she turned to the wizard, gently elbowing him in the ribs.

"We can let you try again if you want. You know, to heal the wound in your ego or whatever before we dive in."

He grimaced for a second, but his usual laid-back confidence returned quickly enough. "No, that's fine," he said. "I'm just happy to leave. And of course, I'm happy to plunge into your tunnel anytime."

She looked fast, stepping toward the portal so he wouldn't see her blush. The bastard had done a good job of coming back from her barb.

Now they just needed to know if the portal went where it was supposed to go. Roland pressed in behind her as she stepped through, and the faintly illumined arcanoplasm, like melted amethyst, closed around her with its familiar chill.

CHAPTER SEVEN

Both the werewitch and the wizard were mildly surprised to discover that more than two days had passed since they'd last seen Earth. They knew time passed differently in the Other, and it had seemed like their most recent training session had been exceptionally long, but they'd never been in a parallel universe for this long.

"Shit," Bailey murmured as they stood blinking in the woods. It was a cloudless day, and shafts of bright sunlight filtered between the trees, hurting their eyes after the endless gloom of the Other.

Roland snapped his fingers. "There must be *some* kind of direct relationship between time in there and time out here," he pointed out. "Since I know we were in there for longer than before. We might not be able to perceive the speed at which it passes, but the Other doesn't cause time to move backward or anything like that."

The werewitch nodded as she examined the area for any sign of Fenris, but he didn't seem to be around. "True. We'll have to keep that in mind. Anyway, I don't see the old man, so let's go back to my place, how about? He knows where to find us when he finally shows up. And if he gets mad at us, well, at this point, it's his own damn fault for not checking in."

"Agreed." Roland almost smirked. Clearly, he enjoyed having Bailey on his side for something like this, given his objections to Marcus' training methods.

They started to walk, but they were far enough out in the forest that getting to the Nordin house might take as much as an hour, which seemed excessive.

So they levitated. Once both were airborne, Bailey focused on keeping them that way, and Roland wove a cloaking spell as they flew over the treetops and down the slopes. The town was unaware of their presence in its sky as the buildings hove closer.

It was late afternoon when they reached the family's backyard. Bailey, allowing gravity to regain some of its hold on them but not all, lowered them to the damp grass beside the pole barn while Roland terminated the cloaking spell. To a casual observer, it would have looked like they'd snapped into existence just then.

Bailey put her hands on her hips. "Don't usually approach the house from behind. Well, make lots of noise as we approach so Jacob can hear us and they don't get startled. Unless they're not here."

Roland ran a hand through his hair. "The ground's too soft to stomp on properly, but I'll see what I can do as far as sloshing through mud and swishing the grass nice and loud."

The back door opened when they were about halfway

across the yard, revealing Jacob, whose eyes were wider than usual.

"Hey there. We were getting worried. And why the hell are you coming from that direction?"

Bailey shrugged. "We took a shortcut."

"Okay, whatever," her brother countered. "Just want to make sure that some demon didn't replace you guys while you were in that…place…and send doppelgangers after us. Especially since I just got back from a short trip of my own and brought some fried chicken with me. Bit early for dinner, but I didn't think you'd complain."

Roland quipped, "Hell, no. I think we forgot what food even is. And if no one's made coffee yet, I'd say it's a Russell kind of day for it."

Russell appeared behind Jacob as the wizard spoke. He was almost half a foot taller than the other Nordin boys at six foot seven and the darkest and least talkative. "That bad, huh? Okay, fine." He walked into the kitchen toward the coffee pot.

Kurt, the youngest of the brothers, was waiting for them, leaning against the wall in the short hall between the living room and dining room. He was Jacob's height, but slightly thinner and smoother of face. "Who are you people? I can't remember seeing you around these parts."

Bailey flicked her hand and sent a puff of wind that messed up his hair. "Shut up, Kurt. Take pictures next time and mount them with a damn caption if you need to."

After the werewitch and the wizard took a few minutes to use the bathroom and freshen up, they all sat down to an early dinner.

"Jacob," Bailey said, "just wanna commend you on getting the biggest bucket of chicken they had along with the extra sides since I'm pretty sure I'm about to eat half of this entire feast. That way, the rest of you won't starve, splitting the rest."

Kurt narrowed his eyes. "We'll see about that. Just try it." His hand leapt out with surprising speed and deposited a breast onto his plate. "Your fiendish sorcery is no match for my highly-developed reflexes."

Jacob leaned back in his chair. "See that? Kurt finally got his hand on a breast. Might be years before it happens again."

"Silence," the younger boy snapped, hoisting a mug of Russell's coffee, which was strong enough to be hazardous to small children and the elderly.

After they'd all destroyed a healthy initial portion of the food, conversation welled up. The brothers mentioned that their dad had stopped by, but was currently out meeting with the leaders of their pack for some official function pertaining to the full moon.

"Oh, right," Bailey recalled. "They only do it every season now. Used to be every moon."

Roland waved a hand. "That's the modern world for you. People have jobs to go to and Netflix series to waste entire days watching. Makes it hard for even werewolves to do wolf stuff under the glare of Luna."

Jacob half-frowned. "You got that right. Speaking of which…"

The girl inhaled; she knew this was coming—the discussion of their training and everything that had happened on her and Roland's end. It would be good to talk it over with her family, but part of her didn't want to dwell on it right now. She'd rather decompress and talk about something fun instead of feeling obliged to deliver a progress report.

She leapt in with, "We haven't seen Marcus in, I dunno, a while. Again, we can't judge time in there. But he never showed up, not even when frickin' Baldur did. Let alone when that other pack popped in. And we never know if that shit is part of the training process or random weirdness that even he couldn't have predicted. I know I can handle it in the end, but it's wearing me down, honestly. All the uncertainty and chaos."

Her shoulder slumped at admitting that. But thankfully, she had deflected the discussion.

Roland quickly added, "I second that motion. After we're done eating, I might have to stumble out to the pole barn and sleep for about twelve hours."

Russell made a low grunting sound. "Tell him."

Before Bailey could ask him to clarify what that meant, Jacob agreed. "Yeah, Marcus—or Fenris, if we're supposed to call him that now—needs to know he can't just leave you guys dangling, even as tough as you are. I mean, yeah, sometimes when you teach someone something, they need to figure things out for themselves, but it's different when gods are showing up left and right and some Weres still think you're the bad guy in all this."

The girl shook her head. "Pack politics never end. If I do end up as this great and mighty shaman, I'm probably gonna have to mediate that crap. I guess someone has to and at least I can bring a different perspective to it."

"Right," Kurt remarked. "You can remind them of that *other* monthly cycle, besides just the moon."

Russell threw a thigh bone at him, but he caught it.

"See?" Kurt beamed. "Reflexes."

"You know," interjected Jacob, "that reminds me. Something else I wanted to tell you, and it kinda relates to the pack politics stuff."

Bailey spread her hands. "Okay, shoot."

Jacob had taken a bite of chicken while she responded, and he spent a moment chewing before he was able to speak. When he did, he gestured vaguely with the half-devoured drumstick in his hand.

"Those assholes running the trafficking ring?" he began. "The cops finally caught the rest of them. Well, most of 'em, anyway. There were stories about it on the news and stuff. They captured the ringleaders and most of the surviving foot-soldier guys, as well as—they're pretty sure—most of the buyers. They said something about how it was possible, at least partially thanks to 'disorganization in the wake of a conflict with a concerned citizen.' Meaning you, obviously. But yeah, everyone's talking about it."

Roland burst out laughing. "Concerned citizen! Ha! They don't want to admit that Bailey and I blew the doors off the operation for them to walk in and do the rest. That'd make them look bad, plus it might encourage the average schmuck to start taking the law into their own hands, and then there'd be chaos. Oh, that is rich!"

"Hey, now," Kurt jumped in. "At least Sheriff Browne sent us a thank-you card and some donuts. Remember that? Those were *damn* good donuts."

The wizard frowned. "I must have been sleeping. You guys ate them all while I was asleep, didn't you?"

"Okay," Bailey interjected. "Thanks for your input and

all, but let's get back to the main subject matter here. Jacob, you said everyone's talking about it. What are they saying?"

He shrugged. "What I just said—that you were the one who made the whole thing possible. It kinda silenced the last of the dumbasses who doubted you, y'know? Like, I don't think there's much of anyone in the valley at this point who still believes those stupid rumors about you."

The girl nodded. "That's good. The valley isn't that big, though. It ain't the whole world. Those guys from down south obviously *did* believe the rumors. Where were they from again? Roland, do you remember?"

"Uh," he replied, squinting, "some creek. Whitcomb Creek, that was it. Between Salem and Eugene."

Kurt rubbed his eyes. "Word travels fast. Well, you said you told those guys off, so they'll tell everyone else down-state, right?"

Bailey took a swig of coffee. "That's the hope."

The eldest of her brothers rubbed his stubbly chin. "Yeah, clearly the dumbassery isn't over with yet. We'll talk to some other guys to see if there's any other rumors spreading or anything coming down the grapevine. It's been a couple days now, and a lot can happen in a short time."

Roland acknowledged him with a raised spoonful of mashed potatoes. "True that."

For a minute or two, no one spoke as they finished the last of their meal and debated whether to get up.

"So," Kurt burst out, "how about them Seahawks?"

Russell frowned. "Fuck the Seahawks."

After they'd cleaned up their plates and cups and utensils, Russell and Kurt flipped a coin to determine who would end up with dishwashing duty. The logic went that Kurt deserved it for his "monthly cycles" comment, but Russell also deserved it for cursing the Pacific Northwest's only NFL team, even if they *were* based in Washington rather than Oregon.

Kurt won the honor and complained all the way to the sink.

Then Roland made good on his vow to stumble out back and pass out, while Bailey decided that she needed to get out of the house. Maybe head to the auto body shop.

"Okay," Jacob said. "Just be careful. You got your phone? Call us if anything happens."

"The hell?" Bailey teased him. "You're my *younger* brother. Besides, I'm the one with the superhuman powers and shit. But thanks. I'll be in touch if anything gets weird."

They hugged, then the girl hopped into her truck and drove off to see Gunney.

His shop lay up a hill near the edge of town, a little way off the main highway that went through the center of Greenhearth. It was now about five o'clock, meaning that the place was still open for business, although if things were slow, the employees might have gone home. Gunney was almost guaranteed to still be there, though.

As the girl pulled her black Tundra into the parking lot, she saw that a light was still on within the rightmost of the three bays, confirming her suspicions. She hopped out of the truck and strolled over.

The older man's voice wafted from somewhere within. "Hi, Bailey. Good to see you again. It'd be nice to see you during business hours for once, but I know you got things going on."

She frowned at that. Technically, she worked here. Until fairly recently, she'd been on the fuller side of part-time, picking up twenty-five to thirty hours a week. Ever since Roland had appeared in her life and all the other stuff had happened, she'd been more like a temp.

"Hi," she replied. "Well, you know I'm willing to help outside of proper hours, at least."

"That's true." He wandered out from behind the car sitting on the lift, a Camaro. "Come on in. Help yourself to one of the orange sodas in the office fridge. You weren't gone long enough for the fuckers to switch from glass to plastic bottles, so don't worry about *that*."

She smiled and heeded his suggestion. Oddly, she didn't drink orange soda (in glass bottles) anywhere else, but the shop wouldn't be the same without it.

Having drunk half the bottle, she ambled back into the work area. "Okay," she began, "what we up to tonight?"

The Camaro was a '72 and pretty much beat to hell. Bailey felt her mouth drooping along with her spirits at the sight of such a beautiful classic car in ravaged condition. It was mostly a dull burgundy color, with white stripes up the front. She'd have chosen a different hue, but it was still a nice model. The front quarter panels were wrecked from what looked like a combination of collision damage on top of years of rust, and the grill was warped and partially broken.

If the old thing was going to have a second chance at life, it was in pretty much the best possible place.

Gunney wiped his big, callused hands on a dirty rag. "I

bought it from the wrecker's," he stated. "Business is a tad slow these last couple days, so I'm working on this one for the hell of it. One day, it might be another gem in my collection, almost on par with the Trans Am."

He smiled, staring lovingly at the vehicle. Knowing him, he was probably looking forward to all the labor that would go into rescuing it.

"Nice," said Bailey. "I'll help. But to be honest, I kinda wanted advice. Things ain't getting any easier with F…with Marcus. I know training isn't supposed to be easy, but it's been weird, not just difficult."

Gunney threw her a brief glance. Then he removed his battered old baseball cap to let his scalp breathe, and his shaggy hair spilled across his face.

"You're alive, aren't you? That right there means you must be doing something right. You can talk about it, but before you do, one piece of advice I'll give is that tinkering with a car might be the best thing you could do right now. Takes your mind off things."

She smiled, and they set to work replacing the panels.

Getting them off didn't take long, and the mechanic had spares ready to go. As they affixed them, Bailey summarized what had happened, leaving out the juiciest and most implausible details. She didn't mention Baldur. Gunney had seen a lot of things in his time and could be open-minded, but even he might have trouble with the notion of a Norse god showing up.

She did, however, make it clear that the training on top of all the pack drama was on the verge of overwhelming her.

The older man listened. He mostly kept his eyes on the

car and didn't say much, but they'd known each other long enough that it wasn't necessary for him to keep reminding her of his attention.

"I see," he commented when she'd reached the end of her spiel. He'd begun sanding the paint off the vehicle by hand. "Here, help me with this."

He passed her a sander and they passed the simple tools over the vehicle, scraping away the old paint. Using repetitive motions was mildly tiring but soothing as well.

"So," she asked, "is this some kind of wax-on, wax-off thing? Sorry, lame joke."

Gunney chuckled. "Not what I had in mind, but close enough. This damn paint *does* need to come off, that's for sure. And getting it off is a simpler matter than the rest of the crap you just told me about."

"No shit," she muttered, conscious of her gloomy tone of voice.

The conversation drifted to mundane things—local gossip, TV shows, and the ever-popular weather, which had been relatively nice lately by PNW standards.

"See," the mechanic went on, "there's always something going on, and it does sound like you're going through a rough spot. You've dealt with everything so far, though. You always do. This too will pass. Just take it one step at a time and let yourself get absorbed and in the, uh, zone or flow state or whatever those motivational types are talking about these days, and it'll happen. Before you know it, you'll be on the upside of half the bullshit, and the other half won't seem so bad."

In fact, they were almost done with the first stage of the paint removal. Time had flown.

"See?" he pointed out. He squinted at the vehicle. "Not a deep sand, but it's a damn good start. We made progress, and the rest will sort itself out."

They whiled away the evening, touching up the Camaro and talking about random stuff. They'd done that for years, long before any witches had shown up, and long before Bailey had even the slightest thought of becoming a were-shaman.

A bit before nine o'clock, they realized they were both famished. Bailey'd had dinner a few hours ago but was hungry again, and Gunney hadn't eaten since lunch.

So they hopped in the mechanic's truck and drove to the Bristling Elk, the town's combined country-western bar and diner. Neither had been there in a long time, and the kitchen was open until ten-thirty on weekdays.

As they stepped through the front doors, they almost bumped into Tomi, the full-time evening waitress. She was a blonde of about thirty-three who'd been consistently flirting with Bailey's brothers since they were in their mid-teens.

"Bailey!" she exclaimed. "I ain't seen you around in a while. And Gunney, hi. You getting something to eat or just a drink?"

The older man smiled. "Late supper. I forgot to eat earlier, and we got to talking and working on cars. That'll chew up anyone's time if they're not careful."

No one else was eating at this hour. *Probably just as well,* Bailey thought, *since the two of us smell like a couple of vagrants who went to sleep in a horse trough filled with old motor oil. Not like Gunney cares what anyone thinks of him. They all know he's a damn mechanic.*

Tomi was along to take their orders a minute or two after they'd sat down. They each requested a beer and a steak sandwich cooked medium for the mechanic, medium-rare for Bailey.

As the waitress headed toward the kitchen, Bailey let out a sigh. "You know, Roland tells me you shouldn't eat meat more than once a day. It can lead to colon cancer down the road, supposedly."

Gunney laughed. "That could be. You're a little young to be worried about that, though. Maybe in another ten or fifteen years. *I'm* the one who oughta be watching my diet. You eat what you want for now."

He leaned back, and his face took on a philosophical cast. "Besides," he added, "I never heard of a wolf being a vegetarian."

CHAPTER EIGHT

"Fine work," she told her followers. "Again, only one minor casualty on our side." The witch who'd been hurt had been on a mission of this sort before and was old enough to know better.

The Venatori had moved southeast. MacLachlan had augured the concentrated presence of lycanthropes somewhere in the wooded hills north of Lake Merwin and not too far southwest of the famous Mt. St. Helens. The pack hadn't taken long to find.

They had been dispersed throughout the area, but half belonged to the large family who owned the farm. Most of the rest had convened here for a full moon celebration. MacLachlan had to admit that was a stroke of luck, even if the rest of their victory was purely due to skill, talent, and the generally higher level of intelligence of witches as compared to Weres. The second training mission had gone well. Her team was shaping up nicely.

The whole pack was dead. As Madame convened her assistants to depart, though, she sensed the presence of other magic moving closer. A moment later, three figures, almost certainly female, appeared out of the forest and crossed the dirt road on foot.

MacLachlan made two swift gestures, indicating that her subordinates should gather behind her but should hold off on attacking.

The women stopped just past the edge of the farm's property. Front and center and presumably speaking for them was a short lady of about forty, probably of mixed heritage, with curly dark hair.

"Peace, sisters," she said. "We know who you are. Our coven is based in this area. Did those stupid lycans attack you?"

MacLachlan sensed that the local witches were excited to see them and more curious than anything. Still, she considered for a few seconds before she answered.

"Yes," she stated. "The werewolves of the Pacific Northwest killed some of our Order and turned the rest over to the authorities. We've come to teach them a lesson and neutralize the threat."

The trio did not exchange glances, but something flowed between them—a subtle shared thought, part of a coven-mind.

The leader smiled. "My name is Janith Ritter. These are my friends and coven sisters, Tamara and Melissa. We would like to offer you our aid and cooperation."

Madame MacLachlan returned the woman's pleasant expression. "Good. You can start by telling us everything you know about Bailey Nordin. You have heard of her, haven't you?"

Another barely perceptible ripple streaked through the air between the three.

"We have," Janith admitted. "She's not local to our area, but not too far either. She lives somewhere in the mountains beyond Portland if I'm not mistaken. The world of the supernatural has been afire with rumors about her and the meaning of everything she's been getting up to."

The witch to the left, Tamara, chimed in, "She's been through southern Washington a couple times. She and her boyfriend, a wizard named Roland from Seattle who we'd heard of long before anyone mentioned her."

Melissa, the third witch, added her own commentary. "They caused enough trouble in Portland and Seattle that some of it made its way onto the evening news, in addition to all the gossip coming over the grapevine in our circles. And of course, the Weres are all riled up over this nonsense about her being a shaman."

Janith cast a brief glance at the burning barn. "They were even more obnoxious than usual."

Behind her, MacLachlan could feel her women growing restless, impatient to move on with the mission. She allowed irritation to creep into her voice when she responded to the local coven.

"We know most if not all of that. Still, we appreciate your offer of aid. Are you really willing to help us, though? If so, then join us as apprentices. That means I'm giving you the chance to enlist in the Venatori Order. The mission is simple—kill werewolves. Lots of them. Show them they can't treat our sisters as they did."

Tamara, who appeared to be the youngest of the three,

giggled. Then all three nodded, and Janith said, "We accept."

"Glad to have you," MacLachlan replied. "Make ready to leave right away. I've got a spell over this farm cloaking the flames from sight and muffling the noise we've made, but it'll not last much more than an hour without me here to maintain it. We need to be on our way before the human authorities arrive."

Melissa looked a tad dismayed at that but quickly resigned herself, her opinion having been overpowered by the coven-mind. She must have assumed they'd have a day or two to prepare.

As the group of sorceresses departed the ravaged property, MacLachlan reflected on her good luck in running into the three.

Her girls needed more experience in combat, but she didn't want to put their lives at too much risk. The more troops she retained, the easier her task would be. Having a few locals on hand to act as cannon fodder would make things better.

It was in line with the Order's overall philosophy, as well. Their ultimate mission was the preservation, advancement, and supremacy of witchkind. The Venatori were the cream of the crop, and as such, individuals from outside the Order could be sacrificed if need be in order to protect them, those more suited to the broader goal.

In just under three and a half hours, the Venatori task force with its three new guides and allies in tow had crossed the state line, passed through Portland, and arrived at the edge of a tiny village just off the highway leading to Mt. Hood.

They probably could have gone all the way to Green-hearth, but there were at least two more packs that MacLachlan wanted to deal with. Those were the one here, near the mountain, and another that would require a slight detour east of the Cascades. They'd still have plenty of time for Bailey. In fact, the delay might draw even more lycan-thropes to the girl's side.

That way, MacLachlan could kill all of them at once.

The sorceresses piled out of their vehicles and stood before the little settlement, which slept under the still-full moon. Janith, Tamara, and Melissa were out in front.

"Right," Madame began. "This is a test. Surely you expected that, right? See how far you can get toward wiping them out before you need our help. We'll step in when the time is right."

The trio swallowed the lumps in their throats. Just as MacLachlan had suspected, they weren't very powerful.

Sighing, she taught them a few extra tricks before she turned them loose.

Nick stared, his face slowly going slack with a dismay that far exceeded anything he'd felt before.

"I can't believe this," he hissed. "I cannot fucking believe it. How could she have done something like this? This is the kind of shit the Nazis did. Why would she herd a bunch of her own people into a barn and burn it? Gods!"

They stood on the wet grass of the farm in southern Washington, gazing at the still-smoldering pile of ruins that contained the charred skeletons of the pack. Sirens were approaching, so they'd have to leave soon.

Marcus put a hand on the younger man's shoulder to comfort him. "I'm at a loss too. Things are far worse than I had suspected. Granted, we can't be positive about who's responsible for this, but there aren't many other convincing options."

"No," Nick protested. "It has to be her. No matter what crap comes out of her mouth, it all fits. She is trying to take over the Were community in this part of the country and killing anyone who opposes her. She's sending a message that she's going to take the role of High Shaman by force, and she has the power to *make* the rest of us accept it."

He swallowed and trembled with a mixture of nausea and fury.

Marcus scrunched his face, eyes distant as though he were contemplating something. "We might be able to stop her by turning everyone against her, but that would require catching her in the act and taking a phone video or some such. But that would mean allowing her to strike again."

The apprentice shaman snorted. "Fuck that. She's not going to get the chance. We ought to stop her by *stopping* her. I don't care what the Whitcombs say, she's out of control. I'll take my own goddamn pack this time and do the job right. We'll hunt her down in her own hometown."

Inwardly, Fenris smiled. Things were working out just as he'd hoped.

Outwardly, Marcus offered a grave nod. "I'm afraid that might be the best thing to do at this point. *Something* must be done, and soon. Make sure you take enough men. If we're lucky, further violence can be avoided. She might stand down if you catch her unawares and with superior numbers."

Nick slipped his shoulder out from under the older man's hand and the two began walking toward the woods, aiming to disappear into the shadows now that the authorities were almost here.

"Yeah," the young man murmured, "I intend to. She's not taking me out the way she took those poor bastards out. She's not cutting anyone else off one by one. She's going to face up to this shit."

"If you need help," Marcus added, "I'll be watching. I will back you up. It's sad that it's come to this, but we need to do what must be done."

The apprentice cast a final glance at the immolated corpses in the ruins of the barn.

"No shit."

Something about having a late supper at the Elk with Gunney last night had made Bailey almost feel like things were back to normal. As if it were old times again, when her biggest concerns were fending off dickheads like Dan Oberlin once in a while and cleaning the mud out of the undercarriage of her truck.

She approached Roland after they were both awake. "Wanna go out for breakfast?"

"Sure," he agreed. "I think I'm putting on a few pounds, though. You people certainly know how to eat hearty. I might have to start politely refusing second helpings from now on."

She narrowed her eyes. "What do you mean, 'you people?'"

He smiled and smoothed his hair. "The Nordin family, a group of people—Weres, whatever—who are noticeably large and therefore require greater caloric intake than the norm. Large as in tall and strong, of course."

"Damn right," she shot back. She put her head into his stomach and lifted him onto her shoulders, where he sputtered and cursed for a moment before she tossed him onto the sofa.

He blinked, then smoothed his hair again. "Well, it's good to know that you can carry me if I'm ever knocked out. Then again, I weigh a lot less than a fridge."

It was about ten-thirty when they arrived at the diner. They'd be transitioning into lunch soon, but breakfast was popular enough that they usually had the supplies reserved and a section of the grill reserved for eggs until quarter past eleven or so.

The waitress on hand was the newer gal, Cheryl. Tomi usually worked lunch and dinner. She seated them at a small table near the center of the floor. Bailey thought about requesting a booth, but it was pretty busy, so she didn't bother.

Soon their orders were in, and with surprising speed given the number of diners on hand, they had beautiful, butter-glistening omelets sitting in front of them in addition to their steaming cups of coffee.

They had tucked about halfway into their meals when

four young men approached them, all Weres. Bailey knew most of them.

The one out front made eye contact. "Hey," he offered in a low voice. "Nova. We want to talk to you."

Bailey set down her fork. "I don't get called that very much. Last time, I think it was by Dan Oberlin right before I kicked the shit out of him. Aren't you guys his friends?" Her tone was flat and even, neither rude nor polite.

Roland, for his part, sipped coffee but watched the quartet all the same.

"Yeah," the leader responded. "Well, we were." He was rangy and strong, if not overly heavy. Two of the other guys were taller and wider, and the fourth was short and stout. "I'm Will Waldsbach. Me and him were friends in high school, but I didn't talk to him much after that. I didn't know what he was doing."

One of the big guys stepped up. "I'm Dan's cousin, Leo Seigneur. I didn't know either. Not 'til after him and his boys were arrested."

Bailey tried not to make it too obvious that they'd bewildered her. Roland too had furrowed his brow and seemed to be searching the folds of his brain for an answer.

"I see," she said. "So, what do you want to talk about?"

The Weres exchanged glances. "We wanted to apologize," Will rumbled, "for all the crap Dan's gang did. We didn't have no part in it. Especially not the kidnappings, and we never harassed you either, did we? We heard about everything you've done, though. And about," he swallowed, "who's teaching you now. How you're gonna be the shaman."

Bailey couldn't pretend to be nonchalant any longer. Her jaw dropped and her eyes widened.

"So," Will went on, "what I'm trying to say is, I want us to be on good terms. Everyone knows you're a hell of a fighter. And aside from some of the bullshit rumors, everyone knows you're trying to do well by all the packs in the valley. Saving our girls, kicking the asses of the guys who took them, and driving off those witches. If…Fenris wants you to be our shaman, then we don't got a problem with that. You're someone we could follow. We got your back."

The other three nodded their agreement.

Bailey took a deep breath and raised her coffee mug for a quick sip to give herself a second to think. "Thanks," she said after a pause. "I guess I wasn't expecting that, but it's good to hear. Too many Weres lately have been acting crazy. You guys eating? Pull up a table if you want."

Roland gave them a curt smile and flourished his hand for them to do as Bailey had suggested. He wasn't as enthusiastic as the girl was since he didn't know the four, just as he still didn't understand lycanthrope society. But it was obvious they had nothing to fear from Will or his friends.

The quartet had just dragged up a table when the front doors around a corner from the dining area burst open and in tramped a group of people. A large group, from the sound of it. Moving fast and stomping hard.

Roland craned his neck. "The hell is that?" Subtle twists of his fingers suggested he was preparing a spell—something subtle and tactical, nothing like the flashy destructive magic he'd used in the Other.

Bailey frowned. "We're about to find out."

A crowd of young men, along with a couple of women, marched around the corner and into the dining area. There were at least twenty of them, maybe twenty-five. Most were large, muscular, rough-looking sorts. Bailey figured most of them for werewolves, although a few could be human allies. She'd never seen any of them before.

They muscled their way in, streaming between the booths and tables, making other diners scooch their chairs in to avoid them. Then they spread out to form a squared-off U-shape around the double table where Bailey, Roland, and their four new friends sat.

The werewitch watched them. She said and did nothing, only waited for them to introduce themselves.

Out in front was their presumed leader. It was difficult to judge his age; he might have been twenty-five or forty. He was of average height, but fit and muscular, with a shaved head, a well-groomed black chin beard, and tattoos on his bare arms, which he'd crossed over his chest. His eyes were cold and steady.

"You're Bailey Nordin," he stated.

Bailey slightly inclined her head. "Yep, that's me. Who are you, and what brings you to Greenhearth? Don't think I've—"

"Cut the crap," he interrupted her. "We know what you've been doing lately. So does the entire rest of wolfdom all through Oregon and Washington. To answer your question, my name is Nick Jezak, apprentice shaman of the Shashka Pack—one of the ones you haven't wiped out yet."

A visible tremor of deadly rage went through the whole gang as if they were a single animal prepared to pounce.

The entire diner had gone dead silent. No noise inter-fered with Bailey's thoughts or the rush of intertwining emotions.

That's him, she concluded. *This is the fucker who's been inciting those other packs against me. But what the hell does he mean by wiped out? Is someone out there killing Weres?*

There was no time to try to come up with answers to her mental questions, though. Nick was continuing his spiel.

"This woman," he announced, his voice filling the whole building as he pointed at her face, "is a threat to every lycanthrope—man, woman, and child—in the region, and she'll be a threat to the whole goddamn world unless she's stopped. She's not fit to be a shaman. We have confirmed evidence that her power, probably combined with jealousy and resentment, has driven her crazy. The result is two entire packs in Washington dead. I'm talking mass murder, genocide. Check the Internet or listen to the radio if you don't believe me."

Gasps went around the diner. The normal humans of Greenhearth were aware that lycanthropes lived among them, and silence on the subject was a long tradition. News like that was more shocking to them than if they'd had no idea about such things.

Bailey gawked. Things were on the verge of going completely out of control.

"What the fuck are you talking about?" she urged. "I haven't killed any Weres. I've been here the whole...time."

As the words left her mouth, she realized she had inad-vertently lied. She and Roland had been in the Other. For all anyone else here knew, they might as well have been in China.

Or in Washington.

Nick shook his head and narrowed his eyes. "*No*. We're ending you right now."

Patrons screamed, knocking over chairs as they rose from their seats and made for the doors. Bailey's four new friends closed protectively around her and Roland, and half of the wolves of Shashka shifted form to attack.

CHAPTER NINE

People became wolves, and the formerly peaceful diner became a melee. The quartet of South Cliffs hadn't been kidding when they'd pledged Bailey their allegiance since all of them changed into their beast forms and hovered around the girl and the wizard.

The civilians scattered, shouting for someone to call 911 as the Weres from Nick's group pounced on their targets. The others, still in human form, advanced more slowly from all sides.

Bailey had already sprung up, her chair falling and sliding behind her, where it got tangled in the legs of one of the Shashkas. He tripped and knocked his face into a booth seat.

Roland was up too. "For fuck's sake! We can't even eat a nice greasy brunch without this shit happening anymore!" At a flick of his hand, one of the bounding wolves mysteriously tripped on a table and sprawled into the opposite wall, missing Bailey's head by at least five feet.

Seeing the wizard do that, Bailey remembered they

were in public on Earth. In the damn Elk on a busy day. They couldn't afford to toss around hyper-destructive magic. This fight would come down to the subtler sorts, abetted by fangs, fists, and muscle.

One of the Shashka men, a guy in his early twenties who had to be at least six foot four, took a swing at her, but for all his strength, he was clumsy, and the girl easily ducked his crude roundhouse. Her knee shot into his groin at the same time her fists pummeled his stomach, then she'd slipped her foot behind his ankle while piling her weight against him. He stumbled and fell, by which point she was bounding back up into the fray.

Another man had been momentarily caught between a failed strike at one of Bailey's South Cliff wolves and a second strike at Bailey. His hesitation was all she needed to sock him in the jaw and drop-kick him into a booth seat.

Then a shifted wolf pounced on her. She blocked its claws and whipped her head back from its drooling mouth, pushing it upward. One of her allies, also in beast form, grabbed the wolf by the scruff and hoisted him off, then the two animals became a rolling tangle of furry limbs.

In the second it took Bailey to get her bearings, two more Shashkas in human form charged. She thrust out her hands and created a weak wave of concussive force, just enough to stagger them. One dropped to his knees.

The other was less affected, so Bailey elbowed him in the face. His nose crunched and he blundered backward, holding his hands to his face to the stave off the blood flowing from it.

Someone else hit her from the side, and for a few moments, all was pandemonium. She lashed out with her hands and knees and feet, never staying in the same place for more than a split second, pounding on anything within arm's reach.

She caught fractured glimpses of people swinging chairs and breaking them over each other's heads, wolves gnashing their deadly jaws at each other, and injured men crawling free of the brawl.

And Roland, dancing atop the half-walls that divided the booths and kicking Weres in their faces.

The wizard knew he couldn't risk burning the diner down, and it occurred to him that he'd lately grown overly reliant on magic of the pyrotechnic sort. Their training in the Other and their arcane battles against the Venatori had left him out of practice at using sorcery to augment himself as an empty-handed fighter.

But his skills and knowledge came back to him quickly enough. He manipulated gravity to his benefit, deftly using the furniture and layout of the dining area to stay out of reach of the humanoid Shashkas and leap away from the lunges of the ones in wolf form.

He levitated hard plastic drinking glasses into his hands, then threw them, enhancing their velocity and guiding their accuracy through magic. They shot into the Weres' faces or testicles, or struck them in the backs of their knees to make them stumble.

He directed wolves and men to trip into vacant tables and spill silverware, only to find forks and knives embedded in their limbs, perfectly stuck in just such parts of their anatomy as to hobble them in a fight without crippling them or making them bleed to dangerous levels.

And when all else failed, he simply jumped into the

open air and guided his fists like heat-seeking missiles into snouts, kidneys, or solar plexuses. Then he was airborne again. If an average person was watching, they'd think him a highly-skilled martial artist or perhaps a gymnast.

Will and Leo and the other two former friends of Dan Oberlin did their part, proving their bravery mere minutes after they'd sworn friendship to Bailey and Roland. Rallying around the werewitch and the wizard, they flattened most of the Shashkas who assaulted them and held a defensive position in the far front corner of the dining hall.

But they were still outnumbered five to one.

The six of them might have had a fighting chance against the twenty intruders if it weren't for Nick. Though supposedly only an apprentice shaman, he quickly demonstrated that his magic was nothing to be trifled with.

Thus far, he'd been tossing streams of invisible force into the melee, subtly wearing down the South Cliffs with a level of precision and control beyond Bailey's skills, or even Roland's. Now, with his targets out of reach but his allies by far the more numerous, even though a few had been hurt badly enough to be taken out of the fight, it was time to try something different.

Nick clasped his right hand over his left fist and held it in front of his chest, and a tremor went through his body as his powerful shoulders shrugged forward and his head angled down. A faint aura, colored like tarnished silver, began to emanate from him, then the same shine appeared around the wolves of his pack.

As the shaman began to chant, the Shashkas renewed their attack with almost double the speed, power, and ferocity they'd displayed thus far.

"This is bad," Roland exclaimed, pointing out what was fairly obvious to them all as he tried to hold two Weres back with a transparent magical shield. "He's buffing them somehow. It's pure were-shaman stuff, whatever it is, so it's not magic I'm familiar with."

The song Nick had begun to sing was loud and heavy and guttural, like a battle hymn Vikings or Cossacks or Scythian horsemen might have intoned centuries prior. In time with the primitive yet mesmerizing notes of the chant, glowing runes appeared in the air before him, rotating in a circle.

And his warriors went berserk.

Bailey was suddenly charged by two Shashkas who came out of nowhere with incredible swiftness, and all she could do was block their attacks with her arms, augmented with subtle protective magic. Her friends had problems of their own as the enemy Weres pounced, so she strove against them alone.

Leo took a nasty paw-strike to the chest, bruising and perhaps cracking a rib or two and drawing blood from a pair of lacerations. Grunting and sputtering, he backed to the rear of the fight. He was still able to prevent the Shashkas from flanking the rest of them, but he was in no condition to help with the main struggle.

The rest of them were wearing down under the ferocious onslaught as well. Unless help or a miracle arrived there was no way for the six from Greenhearth to win this fight as it now stood.

Bailey pushed back against her pair of snarling attackers, bowling one over and getting the other tangled up amidst his fellows since too many of them were trying to strike at once to manage a disciplined frontal assault.

Roland grunted as he fended off another attacker. "I'm going to have to use magic that might get us in trouble," he gasped. "Not much choice at the moment."

Bailey's anger surged through her in waves of heat and cold. Her teeth ground together, and her fists wanted to knock down stone pillars or put holes through trees.

"That's it," she snarled. "Enough is fucking enough!"

Agent Townsend stood at the center of the open floor on the highest story of the Agency's Western Regional Headquarters. It was an unmarked office building, tall but not a skyscraper, in glossy black. It stood just outside of Reno, Nevada, a location deemed appropriate for overseeing all three West Coast states plus the next four to the east, as well as the western portion of Montana.

Besides, Nevada was the traditional state in which to place facilities of the less-publicized portions of the US government.

Townsend's hands were clasped behind his back, and he stood ramrod-straight, his shoulders thrown back and his tie perfectly aligned with the edges of his jacket. His dark glasses covered his eyes and his mouth did not move, but a shining pearl of sweat was slowly working its way down the side of his head. Two glaring floodlights were aimed directly at him.

Just beyond the lights, at a desk on an elevated platform, were the silhouettes of two dark figures. The bosses.

"Agent Townsend," the left-hand one began in a high rapid voice, "the data you've collated is convincing as well as alarming. But before we can authorize any kind of large-scale action, we needed to hear your verbal statement in person."

The right-hand one added, "Standard operating procedure." His voice was slow, deep, and monotonously deliberate. "We must hear you out. Make your case, sir. Do not bother repeating the basics. We've read your report."

The agent inhaled deeply through his nose, then opened his mouth.

"Sirs," he began, "we have a situation on our hands that threatens to upend everything we've striven for continuously these last few decades. Not years, *decades*. If we were to examine all possible outcomes and place them on a scale of best-case to worst-case scenarios, the *halfway point* would still be well into territory that we would describe as catastrophic."

The bosses were silent for a moment, then Left asked, "Are you sure that this is an objective assessment, Townsend?"

"You're not allowing your feelings for the late Agent Spall to get in the way?" Right added.

Townsend was too well-disciplined to react in a blatant way, but he allowed his face to settle into a deeper grimace.

"This," he answered them, "was the best and most objective view I could produce after employing the recommended procedures for emotional decompression."

"Good," said Left.

"Go on," said Right.

He breathed in again and adjusted his posture by an

inch or so.

"It is my belief that the Venatori, rather than merely pursuing a feud, have gone off the proverbial deep end and are attempting to perpetrate a lycanthrope genocide, thereby eliminating one of the chief rival populations to the hegemony of sorceresses. Given the level of violence that's already occurred, to say nothing of what else might be coming in the very near future, I am forced to remind our organization that our responsibilities are not only to clean up messes after they've happened but whenever possible, to prevent these sorts of fiascoes from happening."

The two dark silhouettes moved in a way that suggested they were looking at one another before returning their gazes to the agent.

Left observed, "The most recent data do point to an unusually high level of homicidal activity by the recently-arrived group."

"Essentially a scorched-earth policy," Right agreed. "Ruthless even by their standards. The facts thus far support your argument. Continue."

Townsend did.

"To put it bluntly, we need to keep this from blowing up. It's not just one powder keg, it's multiple powder kegs, each of them buried right underneath the porta-potties at an electronic music festival. When it blows…"

He sucked in air to give his lungs the necessary sustenance to finish the analogy.

"…it's going to be a raver's wet dream of a surrealistic light show, combined with the mother of all shitstorms. Rain, hail, sleet, snow, and torrential downpours of fecal matter, all of it landing on us, the persons who'd then have to clean it up. I'm proposing we defuse the bombs before it gets to that point. Even if, to continue the metaphor, the people who planted the goddamn things are still here and need to be terminated."

Left fidgeted. "Very colorful, Agent."

"Be more specific, please," Right admonished.

Townsend unclasped his hands and made a powerful, sweeping gesture. He wished he were holding a gun right now. Better yet, a rocket launcher aimed directly at the murderous gaggle of imperious occultists who'd already turned Washington into something from a third-world war zone. That would be a better use of his time than standing here belaboring the obvious to the bureaucrats in charge.

"Things are on the verge of spiraling out of control. We have an all-out war between wolves and witches in the making. You might say it's already started. At the absolute least, we need to warn the lycanthrope community to be ready to defend themselves and take preventative measures, with our men ready to step in at a moment's notice. Better yet, in my professional opinion, we need to mobilize and repel the Venatori's invasion. Because that's exactly what it is: a hostile incursion on American soil by foreign troops."

From the darkness behind the two glaring lights, there came the faint sound of breath being sharply drawn in.

Townsend added one more remark. "To top it off, our girl Bailey is at the eye of the storm o' shit. She seems to attract them, even though I reluctantly admit it's not her fault."

There was a brief silence.

"Your case is most convincing, Agent," commented Left.

Right appeared to nod. "We will deliberate and inform you when a decision has been reached."

Townsend frowned. "Pardon me, sirs, but when will that be?"

The bosses replied in unison. "*Soon.*"

<hr>

"That's it," Bailey snarled. "Enough is fucking enough!"

Nick, consumed by the rigors of intensive arcane channeling, didn't seem to hear her, though his bulging, glassy eyes stared vaguely in her direction. He didn't react when she changed.

The girl was drawn toward the floor and the earth beneath it, and a posture designed for crawling on hands and knees became one fit for running on all fours. Her body elongated, her muscles grew even more powerful, and dark fur sprouted from every inch of her skin. Her senses sharpened to an incredible degree, and a blood-hued sheen descended over her vision as her eyes began to glow red.

The Shashka fighters who were still in humanoid form had just enough rational thought left to hesitate, then dodge aside as the huge she-wolf launched into the air, enhancing her already considerable speed and power with subtle magic.

The shifted Weres were too deeply affected by their shaman's berserker enchantment to take heed. A wolf almost as large as Bailey dove toward her from the side, its snout aimed at her abdomen.

"Bailey!" Roland called. "Watch out!"

The warning was unnecessary. With a mighty shove of her shoulder, she caught the beast on the jaw, her speed scarcely slowed. The big wolf was jostled back, yelping, two of its teeth cracked or dislodged. Then Bailey found a foothold on the edge of an emptied booth and pounced on Nick.

He seemed to notice her, now that it was too late. The slowly revolving circle of glowing silvery runes pulsed and dimmed like a candle in danger of going out. Then the massive lupine creature struck him in the midsection.

Bailey felt the muscular solidity of the young man as her head and shoulders butted into him, but in human form, he was no match for her. The peripheral scenery of the diner whizzed past as they tumbled across the floor and out through the back door, finally coming to a stop in the rear lot of the restaurant.

Already Bailey's jaws had clamped on Nick's shoulder, and she hoisted him to his knees. He was dazed, and his face was drawn with pain. In the middle of the motion, she shifted back to human form.

Her jaws released him, but her hands made up for it. The left one twisted sharply in the rear collar of his shirt, and one finger dug into the skin at the scruff of his neck hard enough to draw blood.

She panted with exertion, but also with rage, staring at him and struggling not to end his life there and then.

"You got some fuckin' balls, coming into my hometown!"

Her right fist slammed into his groin. He groaned and tried to double over, but she held him firm in the same position one would use to cut a man's throat.

"My own diner! We were having *breakfast*, you fuck!"

Again she punched him between the legs. "Correction, you *had* balls." She jerked up with her left hand, raising him to his feet, although he staggered in her grip.

Bailey reared back with her right hand, and Nick's eyes shone with sudden terror as a ball of light formed there. Fire and electricity intertwined into natural plasma, an orb of burning death that she held only an arm's length from his face. He was in no condition to counter her; she could boil his brains out of his skull.

Her teeth were bared as though she was still a wolf. "What the hell's going on here? Why do you people keep coming after me? I didn't wipe out any fucking Were packs. Tell me why you did this!"

By now, the Shashka Weres, not to mention the South Cliffs and Roland, had piled out the back door, forming a semicircular crowd that filled most of the back lot and surrounded the werewitch and her hostage.

"Hey!" one of the Shashkas cried out. Like the rest, he'd shifted back to human and lost the buff provided by their shaman's spell. "Don't kill him."

"I won't. *If*," Bailey shouted, "you all back the fuck off and tell me what's going on. Nicolas Jezak, you tell them to stand down, or I'll turn your head into a pan of cherry cobbler fresh out of the oven."

The plasma ball in her hand blazed brighter.

Nick inhaled through bleeding nostrils and hardened his face, making a sighing sound of resignation.

Then, stunning them all, he said, "*No.*"

"What?" Bailey sputtered. "You want to die?"

His Weres didn't resume the attack, though, and she didn't want to kill him. Not unless absolutely required.

The apprentice glared at her. She now realized he'd made up his mind to sacrifice himself. "It's worth dying to stop you. All those dead Weres up in Washington, not to mention most of the earlier ones here in Oregon, have been laid at your feet. A shaman has a responsibility to his people. I'd be a failure unless I made that choice. Guys. Take her out!"

They hesitated. Nick was still convinced of the justice of his cause, but everyone else was confused.

Especially Bailey. "I don't understand," she admitted, her tone softer now. Force and threats clearly wouldn't work on the man in her grasp, and she found herself depressed, almost sickened by the pointlessness of it all.

Then footsteps, heavy yet somehow muffled, sounded just behind her. She spared a quick sidelong glance and saw a familiar figure, tall and broad, dressed in a bulky hooded coat, striding into the lot from an indeterminate location. Weres parted to let him in.

Marcus stood between the crowd and the pair at the center of the scene, about three feet from Bailey's elbow. He looked them both over.

"Kill him, Bailey," he said.

Nick and the girl stared at him. He gave a small, almost undetectable flick of his hand, though, and when Nick's mouth fell open, no words came out—just a faint, hollow gasp.

The tall man focused his gaze on Bailey. "Kill him. And

his wolves. They attacked you and tried to take your life, based on clearly false information that they didn't even try to verify. You were set up, and they went along with it. You can't allow that to go unpunished. *Kill them all.*"

Twenty werewolves growled or spat in protest, but rather than attack, they drew back, afraid. They must have known who Marcus was. Who he *really* was.

Roland, on the other hand, just stared at the man, his face icy and impassive.

Bailey froze, shuddering with horror. Anger resurfaced as fleeting images of the Elk's patrons running in terror flashed before her mind's eye. They were good, normal people; she'd known most of them since birth. Any of them could have been hurt or killed.

She wanted to kick the Shashka apprentice in the face for that and punch him in the nuts again, but she couldn't just murder him.

I can't. The thought repeated itself in her brain. *I can't, I can't!*

"No," she said. "It's not right. These guys might be dumb as posts, but they thought they were doing the right thing. They're not like those pricks who were kidnapping and selling our girls. Someone lied to them, dammit!"

Nick had gone pale. Now, he looked like he wanted to live after all. Offering oneself as a heroic sacrifice was different from being executed for a crime.

Marcus seemed to be considering her proposal. "Very well," he agreed. "The pack will be spared. But…"

Too fast for anyone to react, his big hands shot out, seized Nick by the head, and snapped his neck. The wide eyes went glassy, and his body slumped in Bailey's grip.

"No!" she protested. "Why the hell did you do that? He surrendered, goddammit!"

The wolves were agitated but too awed by the presence of their god to do anything.

Fenris was impassive. "Like you said, Bailey, someone lied to this pack, and that someone was him." He gestured to the corpse, and the Shashkas slowly fell silent.

She searched for his eyes, but they were shadowed by his hood.

He continued, "He was clearly corrupted by ambition, jealousy, and envy. You, on many occasions, have made it clear that you have no desire to forcibly displace other packs' shamans or alphas, yet he continued to spread that vile rumor with the passion of a true believer. Addicted to the reins of power he held over the packs of central Oregon, he felt threatened by your rise, even after I decreed that you *shall* be the High Shaman and none may question it. *This* is the result."

Sirens were approaching. Bailey hoped it was Sheriff Browne and his men rather than the state troopers or the feds or the goddamn Men in Black. Though even Browne might well toss her in the slammer over a dead man lying outside a destroyed diner.

Roland interceded, "We need to get out of here. You guys better head for the hills and fast."

Marcus' hand shot up in a powerful grasping motion. "You may leave, but know this. You follow Bailey Nordin now. She is your shaman. I, Fenris, have spoken."

With grunted oaths and half-terrified bows, the Shashkas backed away, then shifted and sprang off through empty lots and narrow lanes toward the forest.

Marcus looked at Bailey. "He led them astray. Acting as he did is against our code, and a violation of that magnitude has to be severely punished. Death alone could redress the affront he's done to your pack and your town. Now, as Roland suggested, we must go. Back into the Other. Come with me."

The tall shaman knelt and picked up Nick's body. Removing it as evidence from the scene of the crime, Bailey realized. Thinking of it that way only made it worse. Then Marcus opened a portal near the back dumpster and stepped through it, Nick draped over his shoulders.

Bailey stood up. She looked past Roland toward her four new friends, who'd fought bravely to protect her. Tomi, the waitress, had also drifted out the back door despite her obvious fear.

"Tell the cops," Bailey began, "the gist of what happened. I'll deal with the rest when I get back. Somehow. And I'm sorry. We're really, really sorry. We love this place. And don't take it out on my brothers. I know you'd like to still see them around here, Tomi."

The waitress managed a wan smile.

The werewitch turned to her partner. "Come on, Roland."

She couldn't recall the last time she'd seen him looking so cold and bitter, and she knew why. He blamed Marcus for what had just transpired and obviously disagreed with his judgment. At this point, she wondered if the only thing keeping him from heading for the hills himself was her.

"Gosh," he said, "I can hardly wait."

He handed her the remains of her clothes.

The part of the Other they'd come to was one Bailey and Roland had never seen before. Even denser and swampier than most places in a realm dominated by bogs, it was dark, dismal, and foreboding, yet somehow peaceful in its seclusion. A slight rise in the land, covered by dull purplish weeds, extended above a vast expanse of burbling water strewn with floating masses of plant matter. The ebony trees rose high enough overhead to blot out most of the deep-violet sky.

The three figures crouched on the rise, a layer of mist roiling on the ground below them. Fenris had conjured up another campfire from a few pieces of gnarled wood, and it seemed the flames would magically burn as long as they needed them to.

Bailey huddled beside the fire, trying not to get lost in her thoughts. Roland was giving the tall shaman a piece of his mind.

"You killed a man in public," he ranted, barely controlling his tone of voice. "Half the people in town are regulars there, and most of them aren't going to care that you're a god. Either they believe in a *different* God or none at all. If you want to go around pretending to be a human, you have to abide by human laws, or everyone's life will get a lot more difficult, especially Bailey's, and mine. Here I was, thinking you were better at understanding mortals than most divine beings, and then you pull something like this. You're endangering Bailey. Do you realize that?"

Marcus stood, unmoving and unmoved, and waited for the wizard to run out of steam. Bailey tried not to be alarmed. She was pretty sure her teacher would refrain from smiting Roland like a bug for her sake. Still, it surprised her to see him fly off the rails at a being of Fenris' power. She had to admire his courage.

It occurred to her also that Fenris wasn't *his* deity, Freya was. Roland had been far more deferential to her. He'd been cautious with Baldur, who was an unknown quantity to them both.

The shaman cleared his throat. "I did not kill a man, I killed a Were. According to *our* laws, his death was justified. Ultimately, it is none of the human authorities' business."

While Roland threw up his hands in exasperation, Marcus knelt by the fire, having produced a broad stone cup in which he now was brewing some liquid.

"Okay." Roland sighed, "I know there's a partition between the supernatural and the so-called normal parts of the world, and that certain things tend to get swept under the rug. However, this wasn't the same thing as wolf killing wolf out in the woods. It was more like—"

"Like you and Bailey," Marcus interrupted, "running

cars off the road in the middle of Portland and Seattle. Although Greenhearth is a far smaller town, one where the existence of Weres is understood and recognized."

The wizard bit down on whatever his next comment would have been. He was shaking with anger but unable to produce an immediate comeback.

The shaman went on, "Truces exist between humanity and lycanthropes and go back a long way. People will converge on the 'crime scene' and fill out the necessary paperwork to make certain it *looks* like human laws are being observed. In the end, it will be dismissed as something that belongs on the other side of the 'partition' of which you speak."

Bailey knew Marcus was right, or mostly right, but she was still worried. Even if no one was arrested, the Elk might never be the same. People in town might be afraid to go out and talk to each other, like suburbanites in a neighborhood where a gang war had spilled over.

"And," Marcus added, "there was no body. Therefore they cannot classify it as a homicide."

After they'd come into the parallel dimension, the shaman had left Bailey and Roland alone for a few minutes while he took Nick's corpse through another portal. It led to Shashka, Oregon, and he returned the young man's remains to his family. And the rest of the pack would whisper the truth of what had happened.

No Weres would report it as a murder to the human cops. None.

Roland sat down and put his face in his hands. "Okay, fine. Maybe you *do* sort of know what you're talking about.

But could you at least warn us about this shit? I'm just glad I got a decent night's sleep for once."

"It depends on the needs of Bailey's training. And because she obviously considers you a potential consort, I will not retaliate against your challenge. But don't do it again."

Roland refused to respond to that.

Bailey tried not to dwell on that word "consort" since it was true.

Fortunately, Marcus had other business to discuss, and his next words saved her from awkward mental explorations.

"Here." He picked up the stone cup, which he'd placed at the edge of the campfire to heat the liquid within. It gave off wisps of silvery steam, and it smelled spicy but bitter. "You must drink this. But first, let me explain what you can expect."

"For once," Roland snarked.

The shaman paid him no heed. "It's a magic potion, similar to what you'd call a hallucinogen. As it's made with arcane components, it will not hit you as powerfully here in the Other as it would on Earth, yet the effects will be more profound as it goes along."

The girl looked at the mug. The liquid within was purplish-brown.

"You should know," Marcus extrapolated, "that this will be dangerous. It's *not* all in your head, not this time. Your mind and spirit will be transported to a world of phantasmal visions. Strange things will emerge, things which might surprise you, and they will test you severely.

Nothing will be as it seems, and everything will carry some deeper meaning."

She nodded. "Like at the black pool." Her spine tingled with the memory.

"Somewhat, but not exactly." The shaman handed her the cup and she held it with both hands, waiting for his command to drink. "The important difference is that in this case, your actions and feelings will have real consequences for your body and mind and soul. The effects will linger long after the vision is over. You will interact with things as though you were a spirit, but as you remain tethered to your body. Any damage you take or bad decisions you make will impact the rest of you. Remember that."

The young woman doubted it would be possible to forget. Seldom had she been more nervous.

Roland raised a hand. "Wait a minute. Is this some kind of sympathetic-magic scenario where if she hallucinates an undead warrior throwing a spear through her chest, a giant hole is going to open between her ribs in real life?"

Fenris looked up at him. "Possibly."

The wizard snapped his face aside, probably to avoid spouting profanity, and his hands clenched and unclenched.

"Listen, Roland," said Bailey, straightening up. "I know you're worried about me, but I trust Marcus, and I'm the one who's most directly affected. If it's good enough for me, it should be good enough for you, y'know? You trust me, so by extension, trust him. Whatever I need to do to get through this and become a proper shaman, I'm gonna do it. That's all there is to it."

His grimace slowly melted, leaving a faint yet warm smile in its wake. "So be it. Good luck, Bailey."

Marcus laid a hand on the wizard's shoulder, and he tensed for a second but didn't object. "She will be fine, Roland, provided she follows my advice and has the necessary strength. I would not have chosen her if I didn't think she did. All will be well."

He shrugged. "You're the expert on Were stuff. Let's keep watch over her, though, shall we?"

"We shall," said the god. He made a sharp vertical motion with his outstretched hand.

Breathing in deeply through her mouth and out through her nose, the werewitch raised the cup to her lips and drank.

<hr>

She awoke in a world that made the Other seem bright and cheerful. It was a land of blackness and fog. There was only a dark, flat sky like a starless night in autumn that seemed to encompass everything, as though the horizon were lower from the sky eating into it. There were no mountains or trees or any other features that might be called a landscape, only darkness.

Fog covered the ground, or perhaps "floor" would be a better term. Bailey looked down. The mists were lazy and oddly capricious, contorting into new shapes at random and writhing, seemingly for a thousand miles in every direction. Yet they only came up to her ankles.

From what she could see, her body was hazy and indistinct. Not quite transparent, but like an out-of-focus image. Yet she felt far too lucid for this to be a dream.

She was in the spirit world. Nothing here could be compared to anything else she'd seen in her short life.

Bailey looked up and started. Her brothers were there, lounging amidst the nothingness, just as they might be doing right now at their house. Everyone was sitting in his usual spot in the living room.

Yet they didn't have physical bodies. They were like ghosts of translucent blue light, combined with generous helpings of the fog that had been forced to conform to a particular shape. None of them seemed to be aware of her presence.

"Hey," she greeted them, and her voice sounded muffled and distant. "Jacob. Can you see me? Russell, Kurt? You guys there?" She waved a hand, hoping to catch their attention with motion as well as sound.

Then a jagged mass of lightning, a central bolt with branches in all directions, struck right where the TV would have been, sending shockwaves that engulfed the Nordin boys, making them writhe and smoke.

"No!" Bailey cried out and reached for them. A tendril of lightning leapt from the horrible carnage and encircled her wrist and she jerked back, her skin burned and her muscles seizing up.

Then the living room scene and the apparitions of her brothers were gone, and she was stumbling through a void of still-greater darkness. The mists rose to her knees, and after some moments, the pain in her arm subsided and other visions appeared.

Everything was outlined in deep-blue light. Figures

were everywhere, many of them familiar. She held her breath even if she was not sure she had lungs and watched.

People—and wolves—milled around in what seemed like the chaotic aftermath of a titanic battle and a drunken party. Or perhaps a natural disaster. She recognized faces from the town, people she knew well and others she didn't, although she'd seen them before.

There were werewolves, most of them shifted, leaping to and fro, fighting each other and attacking the humans and striking them down.

Witches appeared as well, cruel-faced women unknown to her, slaughtering wolves with powerful blasts of magic. Ancient warriors, many of them Norse like Baldur's host of the slain, joined the combat wherever they could, hopelessly throwing themselves into a struggle that seemed to have no meaning.

At the center of the violence, looking harried and bewildered and on the verge of defeat, was her teacher. He did not see her.

"Marcus!" she called to him. "*Fenris!* What is this? What am I supposed to do, dammit?"

For a second, it appeared that he would turn to her and answer. Then a great wind came up—one that exerted no force on her, only on the vision—and whipped the blue light and dark fog into oblivion, leaving only a clean black slate.

Silence and nothingness. Bailey, confused and unreasonably frightened, trudged slowly forward. No direction was any different from any other; she might as well have been in deep space.

She saw something out of the corner of her eye, turned,

and spied two figures ten paces away. One was a shifted lycanthrope who was familiar as a member of her species, but she could not discern its individual identity.

The other was a woman dressed in the strange leather outfit of the Venatori. Seeing her, Bailey tensed, but the face above the armored clothing was curiously young and innocent.

Both of them were badly hurt. The wolf had had a third of its hair and skin burned off and broken its leg in a fall. The woman seemed to have taken a great gouging blow to her abdomen and might have been holding her guts in with her hands.

"Help me," the witch begged in a wispy voice. "Please."

Bailey stared at the mismatched pair. "What happened?"

"This wolf attacked me," said the young woman. "It needs to be put down. I only acted in self-defense. Kill it before it hurts someone else!"

The wolf, for its part, whimpered in pain. Then it turned its eyes toward the injured woman and growled, essentially leveling the same accusation at her.

Bailey froze, not knowing how to react or who to believe. Her instinct was to take the side of her own kind, the children of Fenris. However, she'd just come from a brawl with Weres who'd had few compunctions about turning on her, picking a fight for no good reason.

It was impossible to assign guilt, and she couldn't bring herself to destroy one or the other, fearing that putting either figure to death would be reckless, callous, and unforgivably stupid.

And if she saved one, they might turn around and murder the other.

Then both died. They slumped and melted into the fog.

"No!" Bailey screamed again. She'd taken too long deliberating; both had been slowly expiring of fatal wounds. "That wasn't fair. I should have saved one of them. At least one! Right?"

She kicked, and the aroma of sweat and peat and burning wood filled her nose. She felt muddy, weedy earth against her back. Her eyes flicked open.

Bailey was back on the little island in the marshes of the Other. A fire burned to her right, and Marcus and Roland stood over her. She gasped and sat up, trying not to cry.

The shaman knelt beside her. "Tell me what happened."

She did. The details were distinct in her mind, like something she'd really experienced. It was not analogous to the way a dream grows muddled as one wakes up and then slips away altogether.

And her right hand had a slight electrical burn.

Marcus nodded slowly, his face somber and placid. "I see," he intoned. "Believe it or not, in the last vision, you were right and did what you ought to have done."

She squinted at him. "How is that possible? They both frickin' died!" She felt awful, as though someone had stabbed her with a hypodermic needle filled with acid.

The tall man gave a sad shrug. "You can't save everyone. By acting rashly to take sides in a fight that wasn't yours to begin with, you might have condemned someone without need or justification. Instead, you let things take their course. They attacked each other; neither was innocent, and both died of their stupidity."

She frowned and bowed her head. "In a way, that makes sense. It's just so…ugly and cruel."

Roland's hand was suddenly squeezing hers. She squeezed back.

"Sometimes," said Marcus, "the world is like that. But you're not done yet. We need to send you back to finish your task."

Her stomach clenched. She'd rather fight the Shashka pack again than deal with this shit. But Fenris had undoubtedly trained countless other shamans before her. She would do as he instructed.

The tall man raised the stone cup to her lips again, and she took another swig. The world darkened and faded, and a moment later, she stood once more in the world of black shadows and blue mist.

Another battle was raging now across the plains of darkness. A veritable horde of werewolves, a legion of them, streamed across the ground. All had shifted, and their jaws grinned with crazed wrath, much like what she'd seen on Nick's Shashkas while his berserker buff was in effect. They plunged headlong into the fray, hides bristling, saliva trailing behind them in the wind.

Their opponents were witches interspersed with a few wizards, magic-using humanoids all and on the defensive. There were thousands of them against *tens* of thousands of lycanthropes, and it was a massacre. A figure at the center of the great horde stood on a raised moving platform like a palanquin or maybe a chariot, directing the slaughter.

Some of the sorcerers had given up and fallen to their knees or were trying to run away. The wolves paid no heed and tore them apart.

"Stop!" Bailey exclaimed. "You can't do that!"

In front of her, a huge lycanthrope was about to pounce on a pair of wounded and helpless women. She jumped in and tackled the wolf, knocking it aside, and slammed its head into the ground with her forearm. Then she sprang to her feet and made toward the leader.

The blue light of the apparitions grew brighter, and the figure on the central platform turned.

It was her.

The girl sucked air into her lungs, hissing defiance at the reality of what she saw yet somehow unsurprised. She flashed back to her first vision beside the Pool of Dark Reflections when her doppelganger had emerged from the black waters and fought her.

"You again," she growled. "This is not how we do things."

The shadow-double saw her now, and the chillingly familiar face split into a savage grin. "Yes, it is," she stated. "I'm the caretaker for our people. I'm leading us to absolute safety—a world without enemies." She laughed.

Bailey lunged toward the clone, knocking barreling wolves out of the way as she went. "No. This is wrong. We defend ourselves if we have to, but we don't just go around killing everyone."

Part of her wasn't sure she believed that, though. Part of her found the sight of the battle thrilling and understood the doppelganger's words. To preemptively destroy their foes was to remove the possibility of being destroyed.

But it wasn't right.

Bailey jumped onto the platform, which was a kind of wagon drawn by half-changed werewolves like the ones used by ancient warlords on rampages of conquest. At once, she found herself grappling with her shadow form, the version of her that wanted to bring this about.

The doppelganger spat in her face, insulted her weakness and naiveté, tore her hair out, and gouged her eyes.

Bailey responded in kind, clawing the shadow's face, kicking its legs and stomach, and shouting at it to give up and shut up and go away forever. They traded magical blasts of telekinetic force and ice and burning plasma, but nothing got through the other's defenses. All around them, the massacre continued as wolves fought and killed.

Soon Bailey found herself grappling with the doppelganger, their arms entwined, her fist a foot away from the leering face she refused to recognize as her own. She remembered then how she'd defeated the leader of the last Venatori band, the one time she could think of when killing had been the right thing to do.

The essence of her magical power formed a long spear blade of red light that protruded from her fist, cleaving straight into the face of the shadow-clone. It shrieked and dissolved into a wispy mass of fog, which blew away and was gone.

Then Bailey was at the reins. The nearest Weres looked up at her.

"Stop," she commanded. They slowed down.

She drew a breath and shouted, "*Stop!*" This time, most of the wolves in sight halted or hesitated, looking at her.

"*STOP!*" she howled.

Then she woke up, sweating and thrashing as Marcus and Roland laid hands on her shoulders and spoke in low soft voices.

"It's okay," said Roland. "It's over."

Bailey gasped, blinking and rubbing her eyes, glancing around to make sure the vision was gone and she was safely back in the Other with her friends. "Yeah," she panted. "Over…"

The men helped her to her feet, and Marcus' hand never left her arm. He turned to Roland. "Leave us. Fly over the swamp in that direction and wait on a rocky hill you find there. I will fetch you when we're ready."

"All right," he muttered, though clearly, he'd prefer to be there to help if needed. He jumped into the air and floated off between the slimy black trees.

After Bailey had had a moment to catch her breath and calm down, Fenris asked, "What did you see? What did you do?"

She didn't want to talk about it, but she did.

When she came to the end, she felt better. Putting it into words, and now safe from the hideous sight of her dark clone, it seemed as though she'd won some kind of victory. Maybe.

To her surprise, Marcus smiled. "Good. Bailey, I'm proud of you."

She looked away for a second as a lump formed in her throat.

"Congratulations," the shaman went on. "You demonstrated self-control and initiative in tandem. I'm training you to be a leader, and a good leader requires those two things. You are meant to stand above them and command them, but in a way that demonstrates self-discipline, wisdom, and good judgment. A good leader is not a monster, flattening everything she sees and acting on cruel whims. A reckless war overextends the pack's resources, leaves them open to flanking strikes, and makes too many enemies. War is only to be waged prudently and in self-defense. The total elimination of one's enemies ultimately creates more problems than it solves."

Bailey nodded, her eyes tired and heavily lidded. "I understand, Fenris."

She did not tell him that there was another reason she'd stopped the killing in the vision.

Roland. Witchkind were his people just as wolfkind were hers. He was proof that they weren't all bad and didn't deserve total destruction, despite the actions of those like Shannon DiGrezza and the Venatori.

She had no desire to inflict pain on the families of the people she loved.

CHAPTER ELEVEN

Marcus had offered Bailey a short break, and she'd insisted on speaking to Roland alone. The shaman had not objected, and she'd left him there while she floated to the rocky hill where the wizard had, it seemed, been waiting for her.

"Oh," he quipped as she landed, "there you are. What did your Jedi-Master-slash-deity have to say about whatever it was you saw in there? If you don't mind talking about it. I have to confess I'm curious."

She sighed and embraced him with a sudden motion. "You suck at being serious, you know?" she observed. "But lately, things have been a little too serious, so that's okay with me."

"Thanks," he replied.

"Anyway, he said I did just fine, so that's encouraging. And yeah, I'll tell you all about it."

She released him after a moment. Then, on a whim, they flew off the rock and over the trees and landed on relatively dry ground closer to the places they'd seen before.

They strolled aimlessly, and Bailey recited her visions. This time, she told of them in slightly less detail because she didn't feel like going through it all again. She summarized the main points.

"Interesting," the wizard mused, his eyes getting that distant look as he turned things over in his mind. "I suppose it's good to know that you *don't* think it would be smart to become the furry version of Adolf Hitler or Genghis Khan. Frankly, it's even *better* to know that Fenris approves of your choice."

"Yeah," she murmured, not sure what to say. "It's just that…that thing I fought? It *was* me. It was part of me. It's not…impossible for me to be like that. You know?"

He nodded. "I do know. Remember when I told you about how everyone fawned over me as a kid? I took advantage of that, sometimes more than I should have… and many a time, I pictured myself doing a lot more and a lot worse. If I'd wanted to, I could have screwed *everyone* over and come out on top, but I chose not to. That's the important thing. Everyone has the *potential* for evil. It's just a question of whether we act on it."

She couldn't think of anything to add to that. If Marcus had spoken the truth about her eyeing him as her… consort, she'd rather have a man who was smart.

A portal opened about twenty feet in front of them.

"God*dammit*," Roland blurted before anyone came through. "This had better fucking not be—"

Three women stepped out of the purple shimmer, and the wizard and the werewitch fell into fighting stances. But they'd never seen these three before. They wore familiar-looking leather pseudo-armor getups, yet spoke with American accents.

"You're going down!" the apparent leader shrieked, her eyes giddy with excitement. She was a mixed-looking lady with curly dark hair. "Tamara," she added, "kill the male."

Everything happened at once. Bailey, acting reflexively on the emotions she'd just been digesting with regards to Roland, lashed out with her fist and slugged the lead witch in the face. As the dark-haired lady squawked and reeled back, her accomplices hurled spells.

The one called Tamara swung a flat plane of highly pressurized water like a giant scimitar blade at Roland's neck. He blocked it and struck it with lightning, causing the sorceress to scream and convulse as sparks flew from her body.

The third of the witches swatted Bailey with a tele-kinetic blow, sending her tumbling through the grass. Then she summoned a globule of what must have been poison or acid and flung it at the werewitch.

Bailey jumped twenty feet into the air and the deadly liquid passed beneath her. She streaked downward, furious that these idiots would attack her after all she'd just endured and intending to stomp them so deep into the soft ground they'd have to gradually dig themselves out.

Although the witches weren't as powerful as the Venatori they'd encountered before, they weren't incompetent either. The third witch seized her friends by the arms and the trio vanished, reappearing farther along the sward and jeering at them.

Roland stared at them. "Who *are* those ditzes? They

don't seem like Venatori soldiers, but they're not anybody I know personally, either. I wonder if Shannon hired them or—"

Before any answers could present themselves, Fenris appeared.

The tall deity, still in his human form, descended from somewhere in the sky and crashed to the earth about halfway between the two groups with the force of a small meteorite. Roland and Bailey fell on their asses from the shockwave, and so did the witches.

Fenris reached out and summoned an actual meteor, which fell, blazing and shrieking, through the sky toward the spot where the three witches sprawled.

"Fuck!" shouted the curly-haired leader. They threw up their hands to block the deadly mass of fiery stone and managed to slow it and divert its course to the nearest bog, but that required all the strength of the entire trio, leaving them open to another spell. Even initiating coven-mind, their magical abilities were no match for a god.

Marcus hurled three spears of purplish-silver plasma. The witches screamed briefly before they were knocked back and impaled, their corpses twitching and smoking in the grass. The deflected meteor sent up steam as it sank into a nearby pond.

Roland whistled. "Okay, then."

Bailey just stared in shock. The sorceresses had tried to kill them, but Marcus' increasing ruthlessness was starting to bother her.

The tall shaman turned back to the pair. "How dare they?" he remarked, his voice lower and more gravelly than usual. "I didn't think they'd be this bold or this stupid." He saw that the portal was still open, so he slammed it shut and dismissed it with a swipe of his hand.

The werewitch and the wizard climbed to their feet. "Venatori uniforms," Roland observed, "but we have no idea who they were."

Marcus stood but didn't look at them, advancing instead to examine the witches' bodies. "Such a small band," he said. "After the difficulty they had subduing the two of you with a full squad, they ought to know better. This was a feint to gauge our strength."

Bailey and Roland flanked the shaman as he glowered at the women's corpses.

Bailey added, "They sounded like Americans. Aren't all the Venatori European?"

Roland responded, "Mostly. They're *based* in Europe but they do have a few members from other continents. Still, I wonder if they're...emergency volunteer deputies. Something like that."

Fenris kept his eyes on the trio of sprawled forms, and Bailey realized he was performing some kind of magical reading on them.

"Yes," he stated. "They are not full members. They were given the distinctive outfits and sacrificed as expendable pawns to provoke us and determine how we'd react. A heartless tactic, but a clever one."

Roland coughed. "Compassion isn't a quality the Venatori cultivate. It's strictly relegated to that one kid from *Captain Planet*. Remember that show?"

"No," Bailey replied.

Marcus silenced them with a wave of his hand. "And there's more. There's a latent spell surrounding them.

transmitting visual signals to their handlers—the real Venatori." He made a crushing motion with his hand. Nothing seemed to take place, but Bailey guessed he'd just canceled the spell.

"So," the girl surmised, "they just saw everything that happened."

"I'm afraid so," the shaman confirmed. "These three were unwitting pawns, meant to be slaughtered. And so they were. *Sane* people who saw that would flee, but the Venatori will interpret it to mean that they need more firepower if they plan to confront us."

Bailey shuddered. The witches who'd attacked recently had been nothing to take lightly. And was the Order crazy enough to declare war on a deity? Then again, they probably didn't know who Marcus really was, just thought him an extremely powerful were-shaman.

Roland sighed. "Well, this is just fantastic. So much for averting all-out war."

Marcus turned around. With his next comment, he somehow answered both Roland's quip and Bailey's unspoken thoughts.

"As we'd feared, things will escalate, but if we tread carefully, we might be able to prevent the worst. It's important that we don't reveal my identity. If it becomes known that I've directly involved myself, it could start a battle of divinities, with the witch-gods taking sides against me and the whole Earth becoming a battlefield for vastly powerful forces. Or the Venatori might start looking for the means to kill a god. I would not put it past them."

Bailey reeled in shock. What Fenris had just described

was an end-of-the-world scenario. Not to mention, he'd implied that he could be killed.

Roland rubbed his eyes. "Okay, so what do we do now?"

"Return to Greenhearth," said Marcus, "and continue your training there. The Other makes some things easier or clearer, but it's not required. There's no way we can avoid confrontations with the Venatori, but we *can* win. Furthermore, we can win in a way that won't involve splitting the planet asunder."

Once back in the mortal world, Marcus took his leave, wandering off into the forest to make preparations. The pair watched him go, Bailey wishing he'd stick around to advise her and Roland wondering what he was up to.

She sighed. "Let's go home. Looks like we managed to get here around dinner time again."

"Truly, we are blessed," Roland drawled. "I think Russell might have to make his coffee even stronger than usual, though. If he overdoes it, we'll have committed suicide before the Venatori can kill us."

When they arrived back at the Nordin household, a familiar though not overly welcome black car was parked in the driveway.

Roland frowned. "Uh-oh. Someone must have planted a microphone in the Other. I wonder if the Agency can do that now? Wouldn't surprise me."

"The hell do they want now?" Bailey wondered. "Probably going to remind us again to stop defending ourselves when psychotic assholes jump out and attack us for no fucking reason."

Then she remembered all the work Agent Townsend had done after the battle in the woods to keep a lid on things and protect them from repercussions. Also, Spall had given his life fighting the witches.

"Shit," the girl muttered, trying not to flush with shame.

Inside the house, they found her three brothers sitting down to a dinner of home-grilled hamburgers and coleslaw, with Agent Townsend seated in the vacant place where their dad would have been, had he still lived at the house.

"Hello, Nordin," the agent greeted them. "I'm sure you're thrilled to see me. The good news is that you're not in trouble. At least, not from us."

Bailey nodded hello to her brothers, then sat down and helped herself to some food. "We know damn well we're in trouble from certain other groups," she commented.

"Correct." Townsend had a black binder resting on the table under his hand. She had no doubt that he'd open it at some point, and she dreaded what might be within.

"Wait," Roland protested. "Did anyone make coffee?"

Russell scoffed. "Of course. We already drank it."

Nodding, the wizard requested a moment's delay while he refueled. He brought a steaming mug out for Bailey as well, then the agent began his briefing.

"The Venatori," he explained, hands folded before him and face grim but not unkind, "have come back in a big way."

Bailey wasn't surprised. "Fuckin' hell. We kinda hoped

it'd take them, I dunno, a month or two so we could prepare."

Jacob snorted. "How do you prepare for crap like that? They practically leveled a mountainside last time they showed up, not to mention the detour to murder that old shaman down south."

Kurt tried to come up with an amusing remark but couldn't find anything funny about the situation.

"Well," Townsend continued, "they're here now, and they're headed this way. A group of them landed somewhere in the Puget Sound and have been working their way southeast, wiping out Were communities as they go. This is serious shit. As near as the Agency and I can tell, they're trying to annihilate the PNW lycanthrope community, if not your entire species."

Hearing the word "annihilate," Bailey suddenly connected the dots. She recalled what Nick had said in the diner just before he'd attacked.

"Goddammit," she burst out. "They're behind all of it, aren't they? The apprentice shaman who jumped us mentioned that. The Venatori killed those Weres up in Washington, then spread the rumor that we fuckin' did it!"

She pounded the table with her fist, causing forks to jump and mugs and plates to rattle.

Townsend's frown deepened. "I'm not aware of any rumors. I've been kinda busy dealing with all the mass murders to be tracking wolf-gossip, but otherwise, yes. Four massacres in as many days. There's no way my organization can completely shut down public knowledge or discussion of something of that magnitude unless martial law is declared. The powers that be aren't willing to go that far yet."

He looked down, inhaled, and opened the binder. Bailey steeled herself.

"I have photos of the incidents in question. I'm only showing you these to prove what I've said, and so you're aware of the danger involved. This is war-zone stuff." He paused. "I apologize for doing this at dinner, but there isn't any time to waste."

Roland swallowed a mouthful of ground beef. "Let's just get it over with."

Townsend pulled out a stack of eight-by-eleven-inch printed photographs. He tossed the first one into the center of the table, oriented toward Bailey but there for anyone else to see as well.

"That," the man explained, "is what they did shortly after they landed at an all-Were trailer park up near the Capitol State Forest and the Mima Mounds in Washington."

The photo depicted a settlement that looked like it had been hit with multiple fragmentation bombs. Ravaged, blood-splattered people lay everywhere, and a couple of leather-clad women were visible in the background.

His voice low and thick with disgust, Townsend went on, "I arrived at the scene just after they finished killing everyone—men, women, children. Unfortunately, I was outnumbered and had no idea they'd planned to do this. These are the pictures I took right before they piled up all the corpses and burned down the whole place."

He added the next photo, showing the scorched earth

and a pile of blackened bones. A column of dark smoke rose from the pyre into the sky.

Roland slowly swung his head from side to side. "Oh, my God. What have we gotten ourselves into? And what are they thinking? Even for the Venatori, this is…"

His voice trailed off, lacking the right words.

Bailey and her brothers just stared.

Agent Townsend moved on to similar scenes of carnage farther downstate, near Mount St. Helens, and a third massacre over the Oregon state line, not far from Mt. Hood. In each case, the *modus operandi* was the same. Ambush the community. Murder everyone with overwhelming force. Pile up the bodies and burn everything.

Bailey looked into the eyes of the agent, which, as usual, were covered by dark lenses. "Why didn't you stop them?" she asked. There was an undertone of anger, but mostly she found herself mourning the senseless waste of life.

Townsend frowned. "We tried. I noted the direction they were headed after the first massacre, but then they disappeared from the radar. They're using highly advanced cloaking magic. I have the regular cops keeping an eye out for anyone matching their description, and I'm trying to bring the full brunt of the Agency to bear on this. But for now, we can't track them the way we normally would. There are small lycanthrope packs that have apparently escaped our records, so we can't just post guards, either."

"Unfortunately," Roland commented, "I can believe that. The anti-tracking spell thing. It's rumored that the Venatori have top-level shit in their vaults, in addition to most of their individual sorceresses being prodigiously talented."

The Nordins were still gazing at the photos when

Townsend showed them a video on a small laptop-like device he'd brought that replayed the last moments of the first attack. Elemental magic leapt across the screen and Weres flew through the air, then howled and died.

Jacob closed his eyes. "We didn't know them, that pack. But they look like they could be our neighbors."

Townsend closed the laptop. "If I have my way," he assured them, "we'll have men—*armed* men, with experience dealing with the supernatural—in your town preparing to repel them. There's little doubt they're headed this way, and it's likely they'll arrive soon. My superiors agree with my conclusions but haven't approved the mission yet. I expect to hear back from them by tomorrow."

"Okay," Bailey murmured. "That'd definitely help. And I got most of the local packs behind me. We made nice with the South Cliffs, plus the Junipers and the Whitcombs and the Shashkas farther downstate. And the Eastmoors since—"

She cut herself off, swallowed and coughed, then resumed, "Since the last fight with the Venatori."

She'd almost said, "Since Fenris ordered them to follow me as their shaman," but she'd stopped just in time.

"Excellent," Townsend remarked. "We don't want a full-scale war between witches and werewolves on American soil, but these people are trying to start one, whether we want it or not. It's up to us to stop it from going any further, and we will."

He stood abruptly, and Bailey sensed that for all the man's seeming unflappability, he was deeply furious and still grieving for his partner, Agent Spall.

"Right." Russell grunted and clenched his massive hands into fists.

Jacob nodded to the agent. "Keep in touch. Bailey's not someone you pick a fight with if you expect to win, but we can use all the help we can get."

Townsend strode toward the door to let himself out. "You'll get as much as I can manage. Be careful." He closed the door behind him and was gone.

Letting out a long sigh, Bailey bent over the table and covered her face with her hands. "Pretty sure things are going to get worse before they get better," she muttered.

Kurt raised a finger. "No murder charges being pressed, though. There wasn't a body, no one said anything, and it seems like the Whitcomb Creek pack dealt with things by themselves. There's an APB out for 'a gang of suspicious young men' for busting up the diner, but that's it. That's conveniently vague, isn't it?"

"I guess," Bailey answered him. "Don't know how much longer before the damn FBI shuts down this entire town and interrogates every man, woman, and child. Do you really think they'd all keep quiet, facing something like that?"

Roland made a sour face. "That's why the Agency exists. Not the FBI, the *other* Agency." He gestured toward the door Townsend had just left through. "Much as I hate to say it, I think at this point, we need to have a little faith in them."

"Faith." Bailey sighed. "I'd rather rely on something a little more solid, but I guess you can't go through life expecting everything to be guaranteed."

Jacob put a big hand over hers. "Right. And you're not alone. Remember that."

The next morning, Bailey returned to her job at the auto repair shop for the first time in far too long. She hadn't seen or heard from Marcus, and after the fiasco at the Bristling Elk, she felt like she ought to be seen doing normal things and helping the townsfolk. Not to mention, it would put her mind at ease to just work on cars again.

"The hell?" she exclaimed, staring in horror at the tires on a sky-blue 2005 Ford Taurus. "Those things are balder than Patrick Stewart after dipping his head in a vat of acid mixed with Nair. Didn't this guy say he was driving up a snowy-ass mountain to go skiing?"

Gunney's sigh of exasperation was audible even over the clanking and drilling from elsewhere in the shop. "Yep. He didn't ask us to check them, neither."

The girl shook her head. "Well, *I'm* gonna tell him when he shows up again, complete with a 'don't say we didn't warn you' disclaimer if he doesn't get the damn things replaced before his vacation."

Kevin's voice echoed out of the pit. "Good job looking out, Bailey. Here I was, thinking you're the Han Solo 'I'm only in it for me' type, but you're being all Mother Teresa now."

Her head snapped toward the subterranean depths. "Kevin, was that supposed to be some sort of real commentary on recent events or an excuse to make another lame *Star Wars* joke?"

"Lame *Star Wars* joke," he replied. "I don't *do* serious commentary. You know that."

"True," she conceded and got back to work.

The day passed uneventfully, which almost made her feel like she'd accomplished something. She kept expecting her phone to ring with news of a witch invasion mounting in the hills, or someone's mother to rush up and say her sons were killed in a slaughter of Weres out in the fields, or Agent Townsend to drop by to inform her that the Department of Homeland Security wanted to talk to her. She'd almost forgotten that normalcy was still possible.

They finished with the customers' vehicles around four, and Gunney let Kevin and Gary and Emily go home if they wanted to, which they did. Then he wheeled the Camaro back into one of the bays.

"That thing again?" Bailey smirked. "Well, I'll stick around to make sure you don't screw up the restoration of such a beautiful vehicle."

The mechanic snorted. He doffed his baseball cap and let his sweaty hair breathe for a moment. "You should talk. You're lucky I let you so much as touch a car of that caliber, Miss I Almost Wrecked Gunney's Trans Am."

"Bullshit," she shot back, grinning openly. "It didn't have a scratch on it."

He shook his head. "Pure luck. There ain't no goddamn reason it *shouldn't* have been damaged, with you driving like a maniac all over fuckin' Seattle."

"Suuuuure…" She picked up a sander.

They got to work without bothering to consult about what needed to be done since it was obvious. First, the rest of the paint had to come off. Gradually it did as they sanded the dull stuff off by hand, leaving it ready for a fresh new coat. But first, there was the engine to deal with.

As they worked, Bailey found herself talking about her latest concerns, and as usual, she found she could count on Gunney to hear her out.

"…and the visions I've been getting since all this started!" she explained. "They've been bad for the most part, but it was nothing like this. Just the reality of it. The thought that that monster was *me*. Or that it could be me if I make the wrong choices. I haven't been able to stop thinking about it."

The aging man nodded gently to show he'd heard as they finished the paint removal. "It doesn't sound pleasant, I'll grant you that," he murmured.

"Yeah. And honestly, one of the worst parts is thinking about what happened at the Elk, not to mention what happened with you just recently, being taken hostage by those fucking witches, dragged out into the woods, and threatened. I don't think I could bear to see that again, Gunney. You or anyone else I care about in this town."

The mechanic gave her a sad grimace, swiftly followed by a sardonic chuckle. "Don't worry about me, Bailey. I'm too stubborn to die. They'd have to stop my head from crawling back here, using my teeth to pull myself along, before this damn car is done. Not to mention there's the Trans Am. Nobody fucks with that thing until I give them permission."

"Good point," the werewitch acknowledged. "Maybe next time the Venatori show up, I'll warn them about you and your classic cars. Might scare 'em off."

"Eh," he responded, "they seem kinda dense. Might just

provoke them to try something. Anyway, instead of worrying about me, let's worry about you. It's pretty obvious that all this stress is taking a toll. I think a lot of that is because you're thinking too far ahead and then trying to take on everything at once."

Bailey furrowed her brow. "What do you mean?"

By now, they'd removed the last of the paint and disassembled the whole front, removing the grill. It made it easier to attack the engine.

"See," he said, "there's all kinds of fuckin' shit we're gonna have to do with this car. It'll be a long time before it's in prime condition. But at the moment, are we trying to do every single one of those tasks? Nope. Just the ones that need to be dealt with first."

For the moment, that meant taking out the old engine, putting in a new one, which it looked like Gunney had done some custom work on, and mating it to the transmission.

As the work went on and silence set back in, the old man stretched out the metaphor, continuing to explain his reasoning in his oddly comforting way.

"With most things," he went on, "it's only the details that are different. Those can be important, yeah, but the big-picture stuff is surprisingly similar from one thing to another. That's why a lot of older people know how to deal with life, even if their experience is narrower than you might think. They've been able to generalize their knowledge."

They started to lower the engine back into the car with a hook, and Bailey considered the old man's words. He certainly wasn't a were-shaman, but he'd been around the block many times nonetheless, and she trusted what he had to say.

"When you think about it, leading a group of wolves as their shaman or whatever isn't that different from running an auto shop or working on an individual car. You've already got some of the sort of experience you'll need. There are a million possible problems. Think of how many parts a vehicle has, and how any one of them could go bad on you and might need replacing."

She wished he hadn't said that since it wasn't like she needed to be reminded.

"But," he continued, "you don't worry about every single one of them at the same time. You deal with them by being smart, taking your time, and pinpointing the issue at that particular moment. Then you tackle that one. And if there are any others, or if the first one contributed to something else, you move on to that one. One thing at a time. A smooth, methodical process. If you can apply that to everything in your life, things will work out in the end. Trust me."

Slowly, the young woman let her breath out. "Thanks, Gunney. I mean, in the midst of frickin' battle, you kinda have to do everything all at once, but I guess that would fall under 'specific details.' In terms of the overall situation, yeah, you're right."

He wiped his hands on his overalls. "I'm *always* right."

CHAPTER TWELVE

It was about ten in the morning. Rhona breathed in and out through her nose, flexing her hands and adjusting her leather armor as a ripple of excitement went through her body. She could hardly wait.

Today was the day the werewitch died. And Madame MacLachlan had put *her* in charge of the first phase of the assault.

There were eleven of them, enough to qualify as a full coven and a magically portentous number. It was also more than the paltry half-dozen who'd confronted the American pair previously. Their orders were to wear down the girl and her wizard companion and to destroy any other local resistance until reinforcements could arrive for the second wave of the attack.

To Rhona, that sounded ridiculous and inefficient. It made more sense to simply kill them both—or wound the wizard and possibly capture him—and be done with it. She knew they could.

And the rewards she'd get for Bailey's head! She would

advance more quickly than any other woman in the history of the Order.

They stood on a winding and bumpy side street that descended out of the hills and led into Greenhearth via a sparsely settled corner of the town to the northeast. It was the fastest way into town since MacLachlan's force had detoured east of the werewitch's home to eliminate a pack living out in the rugged semidesert beyond the mountains. Madame was awaiting more witches, who ought to be arriving presently.

"Rhona," one of the lowest-ranking new recruits asked, "should we remain cloaked?"

The lead sorceress smiled. "No. I want them to see us coming. I want the entire town to see. Now, move out."

They descended.

Bailey and Roland walked from her house to the Bristling Elk, where they planned to do some volunteer repair work, followed by a meal.

"So, Roland," she asked as they strolled past the sheriff's office and a small bank, "did you have any place like that in your neighborhood in Seattle? Like, a local place where everyone went to eat to the point that it was, you know, an institution in everyone's lives?"

He stroked his chin. "Not quite, although there were certainly popular bars and restaurants. This town is small enough that I can see how you'd all be attached to the Elk, since it's practically the only place to eat here, aside from the Subway. I swear, Subways are *everywhere.*"

"Yeah, well," she riposted, "everyone here has been to the place, and all the regulars are locals. Smashing up the Elk is like, I dunno, desecrating the damn cemetery. It's not our fault the place got attacked, but with me graduating to shaman, we have a responsibility."

She'd also asked the South Cliff pack to stand guard over the place and help with the repairs when and where they could.

Maybe if they got lucky, the Whitcombs would send some money. She wasn't going to force the issue, though. If the establishment's proprietor and morning bartender, old Maury Fitzpatrick, wanted to ask for restitution from them, it was between him and the pack.

The slate-colored clouds overhead were heavy and thick as they reached the traffic light in the center of town. It might rain, but in the Pacific Northwest, that was pretty standard.

"So," Roland asked, "what do you—" He stopped abruptly and turned northeast, blinking, then leaned forward and scanned the horizon.

Bailey halted too. "What is it?" Tension boiled from her core to her extremities, readying her for whatever might come.

The wizard's nostrils flared. "Hmm. Probably nothing. A slight disturbance, but could just be a bird flying too close to something Marcus is doing in the hills or some crap like that."

They relaxed for about five seconds before a line of figures appeared on the street above them on the crest of a low hill.

"Oh, hell," Bailey groaned.

A female voice, speaking with a heavy accent, pierced the air. "There she is!" Someone else repeated the alarm in what sounded like French.

Roland didn't wait to see what the Venatori intended to do. He surrounded them both with a powerful shield-bubble. Half a second after it enclosed them, purple blasts of lightning and plasma streaked down from the ridge and fizzled against the translucent green surface.

"Goddammit!" Bailey raged. "They're attacking us right in the middle of town! We're gonna have people fleeing and asking for status as fucking war refugees."

She cast out her hand, and a bolt of lightning of her own descended from the sky to strike amidst the witches. One of them caught it with a weak and hasty shield, but the bolt did not die against it. It did slow enough for the sorceresses to scatter, half of them to either direction, before the deadly electricity crashed into the asphalt and dissipated.

A couple of grocery shoppers emerged from a nearby store, screamed, and ran down a side street. Someone's car alarm went off as the Venatori began haphazardly chucking fireballs and blazing magical lances. Chunks of buildings and asphalt from the street were kicked up in the general chaos.

Bailey summoned a powerful wind to push the witches back and then caused it to swirl in a minor cyclone, disorienting them without doing further damage to the town.

Roland swiped out his arm. "Back that way, toward the sheriff's station. We'll force them to abandon the high ground by chasing us. We might even get some men with guns on our side."

They jogged west. "That always helps," Bailey conceded. Involving the cops meant that some of them might get hurt or killed, though.

Roland maintained the shield and tried to hit the Venatori task force, which looked to be about a dozen strong, by sending psionic waves of confusion and befuddlement. A handful of them slouched, stumbled, or tried to cast spells and failed.

Bailey, meanwhile, kept pumping offensive magic at them, forcing them to abandon attacks in favor of protecting themselves.

When they reached the sheriff's office, it occurred to her that these weren't the heavy hitters. They were mid-range witches, probably low-ranking Venatori soldiers since even the least of their Order tended to be superior in talent to the average rustic sorceress. They were skilled enough to pose a threat, but not on the same level as the leader of the band they'd fought in the hills days ago. She'd nearly killed them both, along with Gunney.

The witches also did not seem to have formed a coven-mind yet. Bailey wondered what they were waiting for.

Then the doors of the station burst open and out came Sheriff Browne, his tall, heavy frame ready for action and a massive .357 revolver in his hands. Beside him was his right-hand man Officer Jurgensen, who was holding a semiautomatic pistol and had a rifle with a scope slung over his shoulder on a strap.

The sheriff exclaimed, "What in Sam *Hill* is going on?"

His answer was an especially large napalm-like fireball hurled in his general direction by one of the witches.

Officer Jurgensen almost dropped his pistol. "Jesus Christ!"

He and Browne ran for cover, the sheriff moving astonishingly fast for his bulk. The blast struck the asphalt about twenty feet in front of the doors and spread a broad patch of flame across it, although it fizzled out in a puff of black smoke shortly thereafter.

The sheriff had already come up from his hasty dodge and was aiming his revolver at the attackers. The air cracked as he squeezed off a potshot, distracting the Venatori long enough for Roland and Bailey to crack through their shield and put them on the defensive with magic blazing in from multiple directions.

Then, as the witches struggled to defend themselves, both cops opened fire.

Four gunshots rang out in quick succession—three from Jurgensen, one from Browne—and the sorceress on the right of the formation screamed and contorted, a faint reddish mist appearing in the air around her before she topped to the ground.

"Ha!" Browne roared. "Take that, bitches. Lead has a magic all its own!"

Jurgensen holstered his pistol and raised the rifle. "Dunno about you, Sheriff, but I'm gettin' pretty tired of all those goddamn weirdos coming into our town and messing everything up. *You hear?*" He raised his voice for the benefit of the Venatori, although they might not have heard him over the crackle of lightning and the rumbling of the earth. "Greenhearth isn't just a stomping ground for this shit!"

The less experienced among the witches quailed at the

death of one of their own. Thus far on their rampage through the backwoods of the northwestern United States, they'd only encountered occasional injuries from foes who were poorly equipped to fight back.

In a blind act of lashing out, one of the women conjured a torrent of plasma knives that rained down on the positions of the two officers.

"Oh, crap!" Jurgensen scrambled to secure his rifle as he ran toward the rear corner of the station, narrowly avoiding a half-dozen of the searing purplish blades.

Browne wasn't so lucky. Older, heavier, and slower, there was only so much he could do, so he fired another shot at the Venatori while struggling to dodge the attack. Burning knives grazed his stomach and left thigh.

"Gah!" he cried out, falling to his knees but then squeezing off a fourth round that sent the witch who'd injured him ducking for cover. Jurgensen ran up to his side and the sheriff bellowed, "Call the packs. All the locals. We need backup, and it needs to be Weres or guys of ours who are in the know. Got it?"

Jurgensen was ashen-faced. He helped the sheriff most of the way back to the doors, then ducked inside. Browne remained behind to keep shooting. This time he hit a witch in the leg, and she shrieked and fell over sideways. She tried to control her magic, but most of it winked out.

Meanwhile, Bailey and Roland were getting the upper hand at first, but the Venatori had good positioning and seemed able to reconjure their shields with surprising ease.

Roland looked crestfallen. "Those chicks aren't that skilled. They're low-rankers. It doesn't make any sense.

They must have some kind of artifact with them that bolsters their defenses."

"Maybe," said Bailey. "They weren't in a coven-mind before, I don't think. They might have just done that."

The wizard frowned. If that was true, it meant their opponents were more formidable than they'd guessed.

Officer Smolinski emerged from the station as well, firing a shotgun at the witches until it was empty and then drawing his pistol to plug away. Only once did he wound one of their foes, and then not fatally.

The battle was reaching a stalemate. Bitterly, Bailey reflected that she might have been able to crush them with larger and more volatile spells, but that would endanger the town and its people.

Then the packs showed up.

From three directions they came: west, northeast, and southeast. Their warriors streamed through the emptied streets, picking up speed as they rushed toward the battle. Their human shouts became animal snarls as most of them shifted. Wolf-beasts leapt into the fray.

Operating as a unit, the witches were able to notice and respond faster than Bailey would have liked, but they seemed shocked, and the power of their individual attacks weakened as they were forced to divide their strength among more targets.

Here and there, wolves fell and died, but Bailey and Roland were able to neutralize most of the Venatori's attacks. With grim satisfaction, they watched as the lycan-thropes swarmed over the witches, knocking them over and ripping out their throats.

It was an awful sight, but under the circumstances,

Bailey could not object. Those women were threatening to destroy the entire community.

There was only one left, a tall, athletic witch about Bailey's age, with brown hair in a Dutch braid. Madly, frantically, she fought on, hurling fire and concussive force in all directions, slashing with a sword blade of magenta plasma at anyone who got close. She was surrounded by enraged werewolves.

Bailey shouted at the top of her lungs, *"Take her alive! We need her alive."*

Roland encased the witch in a shield-bubble, neutralizing her attacks while also protecting her from the pounces of three overzealous Weres, who got stuck in the shimmering greenish light and flailed drunkenly as they then sank through it slowly, back to the ground.

To the werewitch's surprise, the young woman conjured another plasma blade and tried to carve through the shield, still trying to get at her target.

"Goddamn," Bailey marveled. "She's nothing if not determined. Roland, I think we need to knock her out or something. The rest of you stand down unless she gets through and threatens one of us."

"Okay," the wizard said. "You hold her while I try a little something."

"Deal."

As Roland canceled the shield, Bailey created her own, smaller and tighter to hold the desperate young woman in place but leave her head exposed.

Then the wizard, contorting his fingers, caused a mingled mass of vapors to coalesce in front of the witch's face. She tried to turn away and hold her breath, but

Roland kept the pungent cloud where it was until the woman had no choice but to inhale. She slumped listlessly against the shield, and her eyes rolled back in her head.

Bailey nodded. "Nice. What was that?"

"Chloroform," Roland reported. "That stuff that people in movies put on rags and then hold over someone's face. I don't think it lasts very long, though, so let's tie her up or something."

The bloodlust was draining out of the lycanthropes at this point, and although they still looked like they wanted to bite the witch's head off, they cooperated with Bailey's will. Someone brought cord and duct tape, and soon the woman was trussed from shoulders to ankles with her hands also tied behind her back. Bailey insisted on leaving her mouth free, though, since she wanted her to talk.

Then Officers Jurgensen and Smolinski lent a hand in carrying the prisoner back into the sheriff's station.

"All right," Bailey announced to the crowd of wolves, "I'm gonna question her, and we'll get to the bottom of what they're planning. I can't thank you all enough. You've done damn well, coming to our aid like this. I'd like to ask some of you to stick around, at least on the edges of town, and keep an eye on things. The rest of you can go home."

Some few of them looked almost cheated, as if they'd expected to annihilate their enemies and howl in triumph over the bodies.

Of course, there were still multiple corpses in the street. A siren was sounding, even as the local paramedics arrived to deal with the carnage.

The Weres scattered, and Bailey and Roland followed the deputies back into the sheriff's station. As soon as she stepped through the door, Browne, reclining on a chair in the lobby with an open first aid kit in front of him, hailed her.

"Bailey. We have a spare pair of cuffs, the special kind we used to keep Oberlin and his boys from shifting. I'm no expert on these things, but we think those ought to keep our guest from trying any more shenanigans."

Roland gave an appreciative nod. "That will probably work, or at least make things more difficult for her, interfering in using her hands to direct the arcane. If all else fails, she doesn't seem to be all *that* strong, so I should be able to contain her."

"Good." The sheriff grimaced. "Christ, we just had a gun battle in the streets of Greenhearth. People are dead. We don't need any more of that kind of thing."

Bailey walked over and laid a hand on the man's big shoulder. "Thank you, Sheriff. You've always been good about…working with us. Looking out for the Weres. I'm sorry this happened, but frankly, we weren't the ones who started it. Now we'll deal with it as best we can."

He gestured down the hall. "You can start by getting some answers out of that lovely lady we brought back, so we have some idea what to expect next and can plan accordingly."

The captive witch was being held in a secure room near the back of the building. The room had a window, albeit one with bars over it. Jurgensen had clapped a pair of the anti-magic handcuffs on her, and Roland stood careful watch.

Bailey looked into the young woman's eyes, which burned with hatred and a noticeable twinge of madness.

"All right," the werewitch asked, "what is your name?"

"Rhona," she replied. "You do not need to know any more than that. You only need to know you will die for defying us. Nothing you can do will save you in the end."

Bailey could tell that this would prove to be difficult.

For twenty minutes, they interrogated her, posing both obvious questions and ones that were indirect. They taunted or provoked her to try to get her to blab information unwittingly, threatening her with being processed by the dreaded American criminal justice system.

Nothing worked. Rhona remained defiant. The one thing they could glean was that the Venatori intended to make further attempts to kill Bailey, but beyond that, they could get none of the details.

"Shit," Bailey rasped. "Can't we just, I dunno, stick a fork in her thigh and twist it until she cooperates?"

By now, Browne had joined them. He glared at the girl. "No, Bailey. Even though she's a foreign enemy combatant —and wounded a sheriff, I might add—she's still got basic rights. We *cannot* torture a suspect."

Bailey frowned and crossed her arms over her chest. "I guess you're right. Damn. Kinda surprised I suggested that. The stress must be getting to me."

At that, Rhona smirked. "It is not over yet."

The werewitch wanted to knock her teeth out, but she took a sharp, deep breath and counted to ten.

Pounding footsteps ran down the hall and the door burst open. Officer Smolinski leaned in, his breathing ragged and his eyes bulging.

"There's more of them coming!" he reported. "They

came right out of fuckin' nowhere! Like, they teleported in."

Roland pinched the bridge of his nose. "They probably *did* teleport."

"Hah!" Rhona laughed, her face lighting up with nasty exhilaration. "You idiots. It never occurred to you that I was no more than a plant! I spearheaded the *first* wave, and I am being tracked. You will be besieged in the place you thought would be safe. You will all die, and we will laugh over your bodies!"

Browne looked at her evenly. "Shut up, you crazy-ass… ugh. Someone put some tape over her mouth while we deal with her friends. And get those damn Weres back here! We're not done yet, it seems."

Jurgensen was already trying the phone. "Dead, sir. They either cut the line, or they're, uh, interfering with it with magic or some shit. I dunno. This don't look good, though."

Bailey glanced out the window and saw two figures in the Venatori's distinctive leather uniform closing on the building. She thought she could make out the shadows of one or two more off to the sides. The witches must have completely surrounded the building.

Bailey's hands balled into fists. "Not done at all, Sheriff. Not by a long shot. Time to give 'em hell."

CHAPTER THIRTEEN

Roland raised a shield that covered almost the entire building. "I can't sustain a full-strength one of this size," he apologized, and veins stood out on his neck and forehead. "It will offer us some protection, but they'll get through eventually, or I'll get too damn tired after ten minutes or so. You guys really need to drive them the hell off quick."

They didn't have to wait to get their chance. Down the hall, the front doors blew off their hinges.

"Oh, shit!" Jurgensen cursed, picking his rifle back up and charging toward the bare portal.

Bailey was right behind him, and Smolinski fell in behind her, although he remained partway down the hall to keep an eye on Browne, Roland, and Rhona in the back room.

The werewitch's first thought was the Venatori had somehow reached beyond Roland's shield to destroy the door from within, but she was wrong. They'd simply walked up and carved the green light apart with their conjured plasma-swords. It healed itself, but they were able to push through in the time it gave them.

Two witches were right there, poised to strike with their blades. Bailey knew she could not afford to be merciful. She struck the woman on the left with a lightning bolt strong enough to fell a hundred-year-old tree, and the sorceress flew back against the lobby wall, a smoking corpse.

Jurgensen opened fire. His rifle punched two holes through the chest of the witch on the right, and she spun, bled, and collapsed. There were three more behind the initial pair and they stomped in, shielded and conjuring all manner of terrible enchantments.

Bailey expended as much magic as she could to neutralize the attacks. Then, almost not knowing what she did, she shifted. Bending over, feeling her hands become feet and her body become far more powerful, she would have a chance to hit the witches with something they probably weren't expecting. During a lull, she pounced.

Magic flashed and something burned her side, but she plowed into the attackers anyway, sending them in multiple directions like felled bowling pins. Her jaws closed on the neck and chest of the nearest one, teeth piercing flesh, and the power of her bite broke the woman's neck. Then she launched herself at the others. A plasma blade cut a strip of flesh from her shoulder and everything became an incoherent whirlwind of violence, but still she lived.

Behind her, Bailey heard shattering glass, twisting metal, gunshots, and screams. She tossed her head, clearing space around her, and as suddenly as combat had begun, it seemed to end. The witches were beating a hasty retreat out the front door.

Part of Bailey wanted to pursue them and finish them off, but she dismissed the bloodthirsty notion and spun back to check on the others within the station, standing up to change back into human form in the same motion.

The first thing she saw was Officer Jurgensen sprawled on the floor, moaning and pawing at a deep gash in his abdomen. Her eyes widened, and she dashed toward a first-aid kit Browne had already opened.

The deputy motioned. "Bring it here. Leave it with me. Check on them." His voice came out in a strained gasp.

She deposited the kit beside him, hoping he had the strength to attend to himself for a moment while she ran down the hall. She didn't even think about being naked at this point.

The Venatori had destroyed the window and the entire section of wall around it, and debris covered the floor. Roland, Sheriff Browne, and Officer Smolinski all seemed to be fine, although they looked confused.

Rhona was gone, only a tipped-over chair and a pair of plasma-cut anti-magic handcuffs indicating that she'd been there. Sometime during the fight, the witches had reclaimed their own before they'd slipped away.

Bailey wondered aloud, "Why was she so important? She was just a sergeant, wasn't she? And they let all the other witches under her die.

Roland, his face curdled with distaste, looked into the distance. "They've got some convoluted plot in the works. I can't fathom their minds, though. All we can do is try to prepare for anything and fight hard when we have to."

Browne, struggling to his feet with a crutch they'd fetched from the supply room, growled, "There's been plenty of fighting already. We don't need any more."

They checked on Jurgensen. He seemed okay for now, but he would need serious medical attention soon. While the deputies remained within to secure the building and put out the last of the guttering fires, the sheriff, the were-witch, and the wizard wandered outside to check on what was happening with the town.

Amidst the smoking ruins and confusion, someone strode across the pavement toward the group. Bailey looked up. It was Agent Townsend.

The man was stomping the earth with each step, moving as fast as a human can move while still qualifying as a walk rather than a jog. Yet, there was no undignified sense of rushing. He was simply moving with great purpose. His hands were balled into fists, his jaw was clenched, and his face had a reddish-purple tinge to it.

"Agent!" Bailey called to him. "Damn. Do you know what happened? They—"

"I *sure* fucking *do!*" he roared, flinging his hands up. Spittle flew from his mouth, and Bailey wasn't sure whether to cringe or burst into crazed laughter. She'd never seen him like this. *"Unbelievable!"*

Roland cleared his throat. "Well, believe it, Townsend. The Venatori just turned this nice little town into a warzone. The good news is, this time they ran into people who knew they were coming and were able to fight back. Most of them are dead."

"I know all that!" the agent snapped. "I just fucking said. I saw half the goddamn fiasco on my device. And don't get defensive. If you think I'm mad at you, you have no idea how mad I am at my superiors for not dispatching the cavalry yet, and even that is only a *tiny fraction*," he held up his thumb and forefinger pinched around about an inch of air to show how tiny, "of how mad I am at *them*. This was a brazen attack on humans in public! *Fuck this shit!*"

Sheriff Browne, leaning on his makeshift crutch, eyed the man askance. "Could you keep your voice down, Agent, if you're going to talk like that around all these kids? Things are bad enough in this community lately, for God's sake."

Townsend glanced at him but didn't heed his remark. He continued to rant and rave.

"This is exactly the kind of thing my entire career was based on avoiding. And frankly, it's the Venatori's fault, not mine! *They're* the ones who defecated all over the general truce we'd established. Next time they show up, we're going to *burn them at the stake!*"

Bailey grimaced. Tensions were pretty high around here.

<hr>

At a scenic lookout south of Greenhearth, dozens of Weres gathered. It was big enough to qualify as a small park, and it overlooked the Hearth Valley. They'd chosen the spot for its symbolic beauty, for its relative seclusion from human activity, and because it wasn't too far of a trip either for the wolves of Greenhearth and the Juniper, Whitcomb Creek, and Shashka packs.

Bailey had also invited the Eastmoors, but they were

among the packs the Venatori had exterminated. It was the last thing they'd done before invading her town.

Roland had declined to come, feeling that this was, by definition, a Weres-only event. He needed some time to rest and think anyway.

The werewitch stood before the assembled ranks of her people, along with the shamans who still lived, Alfred Warner of the Whitcombs and Fred Grotowski of the Shashkas, whom Bailey had never met. He had been the teacher of the now-dead Nick, and his long, thin face was grim with sorrow.

Also with them was their god. Fenris, in his human guise as Marcus, effectively represented Greenhearth and its packs as "acting shaman" until such time as Bailey could take over her full duties.

Knowing who he was, many of the Weres were dazed or uncomfortable. Yet, his presence emphasized the seriousness and reality of their situation.

Warner was the first to speak. "Yesterday," he began, "emissaries of the Venatori, a sorcerous order based in Europe, launched an attack on our friends and neighbors in Greenhearth. It's come to light that this was only the last of a string of strikes against Were communities throughout the Northwest US. The Eastmoors, whom some of us were acquainted with, were wiped out, along with multiple packs in Washington. Those of our boys who died stopping them did not do so in vain because these new enemies would have done the same to every last one of us."

Bailey was uncomfortable with the belligerent, almost militaristic tone of Warner's speech, yet nothing he said was inaccurate. He'd summarized the truth.

The memorial service proceeded, and tempers cooled as the focus shifted to the three Weres who'd perished rushing the witch Rhona's unit. One was a South Cliff, one a Whitcomb, and one a Shashka. Bailey did not know any of them, although the South Cliff, Tyler Ives, was a guy she'd at least heard of and probably seen around town.

All had laid down their lives, rushing to *her* aid.

Earlier that afternoon, she'd been to a town hall meeting in Greenhearth where the mood kept threatening to veer into panic and mass anger.

The town's human population knew the Weres as their neighbors and had never held any antipathy toward them, but they were understandably loath to get caught in the middle of a war that had nothing to do with them. People shouted and threatened to leave. They hinted at lawsuits or suggested going to the national news media if it meant protecting their children. Who, Bailey wondered, could blame them?

Bailey, Sheriff Browne, Agent Townsend, and the mayor had all tried to assuage their concerns, pointing out that large forces were in motion to put a stop to the Venatori's depredations. The townsfolk, inclined to stick by their own, at least appreciated that Weres, a wizard, and local law enforcement had shut down the attack before any more humans had been hurt or killed.

Any more, since the sheriff would be walking with a cane for a while and Jurgensen had died of his wounds. His funeral wasn't until next week.

The whole thing had left a bad taste in Bailey's mouth. The warmer vibe she encountered here among the other werewolves who understood what was going on came as a massive relief.

It was her turn to speak. "Everyone," she began, seeing a welcome lack of harsh judgment in their eyes, "I wanted to start by saying two things. They are maybe obvious, but they need to be said, and I'll be damned if I don't *mean* them both. Thank you, and I'm sorry."

Heads nodded; they were with her on this. She felt a little better.

"Thank you for helping me—and all of us—deal with this horrible situation. We're under attack, and we didn't provoke it. All I did was have the bad luck to be born a werewitch, and the rest of you did even less. That leads into the 'I'm sorry' part. I'm sorry you all got dragged into this, and I'm sorry we lost three good young men. The Venatori seem to have decided that all of us are thorns in their sides, and there's nothing we can do except defend ourselves."

She wasn't done yet, and they knew it. They waited to hear more.

"This started because of me," she conceded, "and I regret that. I never wanted things to turn out like this. But now that they have, I'm gonna do everything I can to *stop* it. That's what I'm training for, and I *will* succeed. We're gonna get through this. All of us."

The nodding grew fiercer and shouted words of assent and encouragement rose from the crowd.

"We're with you, Bailey," one voice insisted.

She almost grinned like a schoolgirl, but this wasn't the occasion for that. "Thank you again. I...well, public speaking isn't my forte, and I don't have much else to say. We'll all be in touch, though. Take care."

Bailey stepped back, feeling as if her speech had gone out with a whimper instead of a bang, yet no one seemed disappointed or mocking or angry. She let out a big slow breath.

Then Fenris stepped forward. "My children," he opened, his deep gravelly voice more resonant than usual, perhaps supernaturally augmented. "I have little to add. Your shamans have said what needed to be said. Provided you do not defy my will or my commands, you have my support. You know who I am, and therefore, you must understand that I cannot intervene directly in this situation without drawing unwanted attention to us all. I will do what I can. Namely, I will finish training Bailey for her role as High Shaman. Soon she'll be ready, and you will have a protector. Now, return to your homes, and make ready for whatever might come."

Bowing their heads in deference, the Weres dispersed. Some went to the vehicles they'd used to carpool. Others climbed the hills or went down the cliffs or disappeared into the woods on foot.

Out of the tangle, the three Nordin boys appeared. Bailey approached them with a faint yet warm smile. "What are you miscreants doing here?" she asked. "Instead of sitting around watching football and drinking beer?"

"Oh, you know," Kurt opened. "Just our god summoning us to a low-key war council or something."

Jacob smacked the back of his brother's head. "Something like that, yeah. Anyway, Bailey, that was a good speech, seriously. Maybe not polished like what you'd hear from a politician, but good enough for us. People are behind you. I don't think anyone thinks it's your fault, and if they do, at least they understand that we're all in this together."

She hugged him. "Yeah, that about sums it up. I mean, shit, it *is* my fault. But how the hell was I supposed to know that a bunch of damn witches in Europe who I never heard of would randomly decide we need to be wiped out just because I rescued some kidnapped girls and then started trying to control my powers? Which, by the way, I didn't ask for? Goddamn!"

Her brothers just shrugged.

"You weren't," said Jacob. "No one could have predicted that. Now come on, let's go home and get something to eat, and then get around to that football-watching and beer-drinking you mentioned."

Finally, she allowed herself a full grin. "Sounds good to me."

When they reached the truck, however, Marcus appeared out of nowhere beside them. All four stopped and looked at him, awaiting his words.

"Bailey," he intoned. "Once again, I am proud of you. You handled today's duties well."

She gave a single nod, almost a bow. "Thank you, Fenris. I won't lie, I was worried. Part of me still feels like I'm the one to blame for all this shit."

He shook his head. "Only in the most indirect and abstract sense. You did not draw first blood. Since things have reached this point, with the conflict having escalated to open combat in the streets, you've done just the job that a shaman is supposed to do. You helped protect the humans in your town as well as the Weres. That has made them more amenable to you, even if some of them are in a low-level panic. You fought well, made good use of your allies, and turned back the threat. It's tragic that three Weres died, but far more would have perished if the Venatori had been left unopposed."

Russell surprised them by entering the discussion. "Yeah," he growled. "They *won't* be unopposed, though." His clenched fist looked like a giant war-hammer from the Dark Ages.

Marcus glanced at him. "Yes. We are a warlike people. Even the wolves farther north who were ambushed and murdered in their beds tried to fight back. And now they no longer have the element of surprise."

The day had waned; the sun had set. Bailey briefly pondered if Townsend's Agency was finally prepared to send their support. It had been days since he'd pledged their aid.

"One more thing," said Fenris. "Part of why the witches can no longer take us unaware is because of the work you've done rallying the whole community. Not only fighting, but also talking to them in peace, and soothing hearts when lives were lost. I heard several of them in today's crowd talking about how you went to the funerals of the Junipers who died in the Other weeks past. Things like that form the other half of what makes a true leader."

He laid a hand on her shoulder, and she put her own hand atop it and closed her eyes.

CHAPTER FOURTEEN

Neither the Venatori nor the Agency showed up the following morning, but everyone knew it would only be a matter of time. They could do little but wait, hoping the Agency's personnel would arrive first.

But they knew better than to rely on others. Defending their community was up to them.

Bailey spent an hour talking to Weres and humans alike and ensuring that patrols of local militia were guarding the whole of the Hearth Valley. Then, with the precious time they still had before the next battle flared up, Marcus took her and Roland once more into the Other to complete their training.

They stepped out of the cool rushing void between one end of the purple gateway and the other and found themselves on the rocky ledge rising from the middle of the vast, swampy dark lake where they'd been last time. Marcus hadn't told them what to expect yet, but the mere fact they were here suggested that more interactive dream visions were on the agenda.

Bailey said as much to her teacher.

"Yes," he confirmed. "You made progress last time, but there are a couple more tests. They are much like the ones you dealt with before, and the same rules apply. Anything that happens in the spirit realm will have direct consequences for you in this one and on Earth—anywhere your body can exist. Do you understand?"

She put her hands on her hips and inclined her head. "I do. And even though it wasn't exactly pleasant last time, I dealt with it. Let's get it over with."

"Soon," the god-shaman replied, but rather than admonishing her impatience, he seemed pleased by her enthusiasm since a smile crept to the corners of his mouth. "For now, relax."

She reclined on the damp rock. Roland sat beside her, while Marcus again conjured a cozy orange campfire and brewed the strange hallucinogenic drink in a stone mug. It seemed odd that a deity would need to go through the motions of a primitive procedure to produce the stuff. She would have thought he'd just be able to conjure it. But perhaps the fire and the stone vessel served some ancient symbolic purpose.

Roland took her hand. "You're going to do great, and we'll be here to keep an eye on you." His eyes went distant. "I ought to be back in town keeping an eye on all *that*, but it seems like having me around helps you. When you're the queen of the wolves or whatever, make sure to shower me with riches and titles and honors, all of which I deserve."

She ruffled his hair and pushed his head away in the same motion. "Shut up. Cocky bastard. The reason you're good to have around is that it inspires me to be less of a dick than you are."

The quip came out sounding harsher than she'd intended. "Sorry. That was a joke."

"Oh, I'm aware." He didn't look offended, although he immediately put his hair back in order. "I don't think I'm that much of a dick, though. Well, metaphorically speaking, anyway. If we're talking literal—"

"*No!*" Bailey cut him off, biting her tongue to keep from breaking into a goofy smile. "We're not."

Not yet, anyway, she mused, then stopped thinking too hard about that.

Fenris ignored their discussion and turned to the girl, holding the stone cup with its steaming liquid. "Drink. And take care. You know what's at stake."

She accepted the beverage, raised it to her lips, and felt the world around her melt into blackness.

After an indeterminate amount of time that might have been a few seconds or a few months, she woke up standing on her feet in a misty and featureless blue-black void, much like the one she'd been in before.

A chill of dread struck her—not because of any particular foreboding element, but because there was nothing. That meant that anything might pop out, perhaps something even worse than what she'd previously seen.

The blue-white fog began to coalesce into figures, landscapes, and activity, a solid and living *scene.*

There were vague humanoid forms that moved slowly at first, then faster. Then came rolling land and roads and trees and buildings and something that suggested a sky. It was horribly familiar because it was Greenhearth two days ago, during the siege of the Venatori.

Bailey recognized herself and Roland by the sheriff's station. Above them on the ridge was the witch Rhona, surrounded by her aides. This time, though, things were different.

"No," Bailey murmured. "*Wait.*" She reached out to herself and her companion.

The other her, the phantom her, and the phantom Roland were unaware of their nemeses. Blindly and stupidly, they walked into the sheriff's office. Behind them, the witches descended. Rhona's group surrounded the building, while onlookers drifted by and watched them with deer-in-the-headlights expressions of slack-jawed curiosity.

"*No!*" Bailey cried. Although she knew abstractly that this was an illusion, something about the imagery was intensely real.

She felt like she was trapped and invisible, forced to watch an alternate version of a reality that was truly happening. A Greenhearth where no one knew what was coming and blindly stumbled into the slaughter.

Then the second wave of witches arrived, the reinforcements. They joined the first group, and a small army began the attack. The station went up in flames before any of the people within—including her and Roland—could react or defend themselves. Random blasts of magic leapt out at the bystanders, cutting them down and tearing them apart. Screams echoed and smoke wafted.

And Bailey could do nothing.

She struggled against the blockage, the unseen limitation that had been placed on her ability to act. Frantic rage welled up as the building slowly burned down and the witches continued to blast it, occasionally pausing to murder anyone who showed up.

Soon the walls collapsed, and within the ravaged shell of the station sprawled the corpses of Browne, Jurgensen, and Smolinski. The other Bailey and the other Roland had severe burns and abrasions and were on the verge of collapse, weakly trying to defend themselves as the sorceresses closed in.

Then a storm of magic fell atop them, and the Venatori cackled in victory.

"*No!*" Bailey screamed, loud enough that it echoed. The sound shattered the barrier around her.

Suddenly, she could act again—at the price of being inserted into the scene, where her alternate self had just been.

She was on her knees, burning ruins around her. Her enemies completely encircled her and laughed at her misery.

Rhona smirked and jeered. "Surrender, and we might let you live."

All at once, she realized that *she* was the one who had failed—not the hapless spectral doppelganger, but the real her. She had lost everyone she cared about. They were all dead around her, the whole town having been annihilated.

She sprang to her feet, volcanic with anger, forgetting her panic and weakness. "How *dare* you! I'll never fucking surrender to you!"

The very fabric of reality tore asunder as she channeled more magic than she'd ever managed before, more than she would have thought possible. A tidal wave of elements and arcane essence and invisible forces descended upon the witches, wiping them out of existence.

Avenging the slain.

Then it was over, and she awoke in the swamp, gasping. The placid face of Marcus and the worried eyes of Roland hung over her.

The shaman was first to speak. "What happened?"

She told him. Even talking about it was painful-not only the horror of the vision, but also the sense that it had only occurred because she'd screwed up. It had seemed like the kind of illusion that would only manifest after a failure on her part.

Fenris only offered a calm nod. "Good," he praised her. "It's just like a wolf to keep fighting no matter how unbalanced the odds are or how overwhelming the opposition seems. The vision showed that you will never give up and that you possess hidden reserves of power. You used them to gain retribution for those who were killed and neutralize the threat. If it had been real, those witches would not have harmed any other settlements after your town."

She sighed and shut her eyes for a moment. "Yeah. True. I didn't think of it that way. Just seemed like it never should've gotten to that point."

Her teacher went on. "You must realize you've been holding back. The power you called upon in the vision exceeded any you've ever employed, and it was unlocked by your anger. Good, righteous anger, justified by the innocent people of your town who were wrongly killed. A shaman must be able to tap into that kind of fury when it's needed. It can provide a tremendous boost and turn the tide of a seemingly hopeless battle. But you must be in control of it. Power like that can't just be thrown around willy-nilly whenever you feel mildly threatened."

She rubbed her eyes. "I understand. I'm not sure I *want* to be that angry. Ever. But I guess it's good to know I can still win, even in a god-awful situation like that."

Roland chimed in, "I think the visions are testing how you respond to worst-case scenarios. You're right in that it shouldn't come to the point of things being that terrible, but it helps to have a notion of how you'd deal with it. Just in case."

"Makes sense," she acceded.

Marcus had gone back to the fire and was reheating the remaining broth in the stone cup. He offered her the mug again. "Drink. You have at least one more trial. Then we'll see."

She didn't know what that meant, but she sucked in her breath, took another swig, and returned to the realm of darkness.

This time, it seemed that the period of formless black was over quicker. The nightmarish illusions took shape almost as soon as she realized she was no longer in the Other. The vision that presented itself was not as dramatically violent as the previous one, but in some ways, it was even worse.

Roland was a captive of the Venatori. He was on his knees, bound hand and foot, his head bowed and his mouth gagged. He occupied a lighted square of tile floor within a dim stone hallway with arches and tapestries, like something in a medieval castle or a cathedral.

A procession of witches was lined up before him and moving past. Bailey knew who they were, although they were now dressed in dark burgundy robes rather than leather suits. Each had a curved silver knife and a chalice that looked like it was made of bone.

She tried to reach out, to warn him or free him, but once again, it seemed like she was locked away someplace where she could only observe.

One by one, the witches approached the captive wizard, cut him somewhere on his body with their knives, and took a little of his blood in their grisly cups. He winced with each slash and seemed to sag after a dozen had bled him, growing weaker with each wound. He was dying.

Then Bailey saw herself. She was thousands of miles away—still in Oregon, while Roland was a prisoner in France. She was leading her Weres, managing them and aiding them, organizing the lycanthropic community in the Pacific Northwest. Doing a good job.

And yet, she was doing nothing. Nothing for Roland.

"No, goddammit!" she protested.

In this vision, the Venatori had succeeded in part of their goal. They'd failed to kill *her* and they'd been repelled from the United States, but they'd claimed a prize to take home with them.

She gaped in horror as Roland, now infinitely far away, slumped to the floor and turned white.

Suddenly she was furious that the spirit world would dream up a thing like that. It was mocking her, forcing her into a scenario she would never accept in real life.

So she rejected it altogether. The imagery vanished like a cloud of smoke dispersed by a strong wind, but Bailey didn't stop there. She refused to let it reform into whatever nightmare it saw fit. Instead, *she* repainted the scene.

In accordance with her will, the mists returned and formed a new scene. In this one, Roland was still a captive within the castle of the sorceresses somewhere in Western Europe. But this time, everything else was different.

Bailey was still a leader of wolves, and she led them on a daring rescue mission over the American continent, then the Atlantic Ocean, plunging into the homeland of their foes. They located the mysterious estate in France and prepared to assault it.

Grimly satisfied with her handiwork, the girl watched as she commanded her Weres to scout, neutralize sentries, and finally storm the great hall, killing the witches before they could drain her beloved and losing none of her warriors in the process.

Then she picked up one of the fallen silver knives, and with it, cut the wizard's bonds. He rose to his feet again and she embraced him. Then they kissed with a passion that was almost as embarrassing as it was beautiful while the wolves cheered. They were victorious.

Bailey felt herself crying with relief and joy. Then she blinked, and the spirit realm was gone. She was sitting up on the ledge with the shaman and the wizard beside her and tears stung her cheeks even in the Other.

"Oh, gods," she gasped. "It's over. We…I did it. I think."

Marcus raised an eyebrow, and Roland was curious too. She told them everything except the kissing part; she somehow felt she ought to leave that out.

When she finished, Roland, of course, had to toss in his

two cents. "Well, glad to know I was saved by a girl. Thanks, though. I appreciate it."

Ignoring him, she looked at Fenris.

The deity, father of her kind, did not speak for a while. He only looked at her with a neutral intensity, crouched before her, and sat back on his haunches, seemingly deep in thought.

She couldn't take the delay anymore. *After all I just went through*, she thought, *I damn well deserve an answer without a lot of dramatic-ass pauses.*

"What does it mean?" she asked. "Tell me."

Marcus took a long, slow breath. "It means that you are my apprentice."

The words hung in the air, and she discovered she didn't mind the dramatic pause after all.

"Oh." She gulped. "Well, shit. That's great."

He smiled. "Yes. Yes, it is. Well done, Bailey. You have passed the last of the tests, and now your true journey toward being the High Shaman begins."

There was a twitter of annoyance in her gut at that. She'd forgotten she wasn't a full apprentice.

"In that last vision," Marcus continued, "not only did you use the skills you'd learned up to this point, but you also showed great mental fortitude and creative, out-of-the-box thinking. Not many would have come up with the idea to, we'll say, rewrite the script of the vision to suit your goals. With that triumph, you have completed the spiritual development necessary to move on."

Roland clapped her on the shoulder. "See? I knew you could do it. And of course, saving me was the final and most important thing. I'm flattered."

She squinted at him. "Yeah, yeah. Keep flattering your-self, because that wasn't my intention. I do kinda like you, though."

"Awww," he shot back. "I mostly tolerate you too. Just kidding. I'm truly, sincerely, legitimately overjoyed for you."

He wasn't jumping up and down, but he meant it. She could tell. There was a kind of warm, beaming energy passing between them.

Fenris raised a hand, fingers outspread, and began counting them off as he summarized all that had occurred.

"You've shown you can perform as a shaman. You didn't compromise or allow yourself to be corrupted by the temptations of excessive bloodlust, greed, apathy, or fear. You've demonstrated compassion as well as ferocious courage in the face of adversity. Finally, you've shown me that when necessary, you can break seemingly unbreakable rules if that's what it takes to succeed. Truly amazing, Bailey. My congratulations."

She blushed. "Thank you, Fenris. You've been a great teacher. I wouldn't have come half as far without you. I mean, you are a god and all, but still. You know how to talk to a simple country girl in a way she can understand. I don't think most deities could do that."

He let out a dry chuckle. "Thank you, too, for sticking it out. And now, I think the two of you need some time to rest and talk. This has been trying for Roland too, given how much he cares about you. I'll take my leave. You'll see me again when the time is right, however. Just be watchful. The next phase of the conflict can't be far off."

After a short search, they'd found what might well be the coziest spot in the whole of a distinctly foreboding dimension.

Roland snapped his fingers as he looked around. "You know what this reminds me of? That motel room we got in Portland our first night out of Greenhearth. Which was… shit, the first day we knew each other, wasn't it? I still think about that. Going out for dinner. Walking through the park and all. Perhaps it doesn't seem too exciting or glamorous, but it was nice."

Hearing him say that, something within her melted. In a good way.

"It sure was a day that changed my whole life," she responded. "And y'know, please don't think I blame you for all the crap that's happened. It wasn't your fault. I wouldn't trade it for, well, not knowing you."

She tried not to blush as Roland reclined on the thick carpet of surprisingly dry moss. The magical flame they'd conjured for lighting bathed the whole of the little cave in warm light. She slipped her feet out of her boots, not caring if they smelled sweaty.

After Bailey's confirmation as an apprentice shaman, Marcus had stepped through a portal and closed it behind him with no further words. Shrugging, Bailey and Roland had drifted over the swampy lake and the woods surrounding it before coming to a more pleasant stretch of forest that they felt was the right place for them to unwind.

The trees here were more gray than black, and they'd sprouted a little bit of greenery, as though spring had come to this spot while the rest of the Other languished in a dead and misty winter.

The cave's entrance lay between two thick trunks, mostly hidden from sight by the twisting wood as well as a hanging curtain of vines. Within, the stone was clean and covered with emerald moss.

Roland wasn't looking directly at her, but he seemed cognizant of everything going on around them, peaceful though it was.

"I wouldn't trade it either," he stated. "You're the most interesting person I've met, and I'd feel...incomplete without you around. I mean that. I'm aware that I'm a smartass a lot of the time, so do me a favor and believe me when I say I'm being sincere."

"Hmm." She considered, making an exaggerated thinking face. "I *guess* I could do that much for you."

"Good." He loosened his collar. "Since Fenris said that thing about me being your consort, I couldn't help thinking what a good idea that was. And certain other comments I've made... Those were sincere in a way, too. Not that I think you'd be surprised to hear that."

She looked at the ground sharply. "Like, 'I'm happy to plunge into your tunnel anytime.' I remember that one, boy. You're lucky I didn't..."

She trailed off, suddenly tired of games.

"Fuck it," she said. "Come here."

He stood up, walked partway over to her, then grabbed her by the collar of her shirt, pulling her straight up into him. Before either knew exactly what was happening, their faces were pressed together, mouths entwined in a kiss that seemed like it had been delayed for far too long.

They stayed like that for what would have been many minutes in Earth time. Here in the arcane realm, it could have lasted forever.

Their lips parted, and they touched foreheads. The warmth and the welcome connection like bright electricity that had always existed between them were stronger than ever.

"Roland," Bailey breathed. "I think…now…"

He kissed her again, and his hands closed on her breasts. "Yes."

She almost panicked. "I've never, uh, done this. I'm not sure how I'll…you know…"

"Don't worry," he reassured her and lowered her to the bed of moss. "I'll show you. Otherwise, just do what comes naturally. It's what you want, and it's definitely what I want."

Too many emotions hit her at once, but all of them were good, and she almost cried. They pressed together again. "Okay," she whispered.

CHAPTER FIFTEEN

Fenris still hadn't returned. Bailey had mentioned to him earlier that they'd figured out how to open portals themselves, so there was no reason to expect he'd get mad at them for heading back home of their own volition.

They stepped through the glowing purple doorway and found themselves on the wooded slopes just beyond the Nordins' backyard. It was earlier in the day than they'd expected; about 8:15 a.m. It would be a short walk home. Jacob at least ought to be up, and possibly the other two as well.

Bailey almost wished they'd opened a portal farther out in the mountains. The two of them had a lot to talk about, and it was better said in private.

She cleared her throat as they started down the hill. "So," she began, "um, well, I'm happy. That sounds lame but I dunno what else to say. I'm not the poetic type. Happy about what happened, I mean. Happy with *us*."

Roland just smiled. He put an arm around her shoulder

and leaned over to plant a kiss on her forehead. "Good. And ditto. I'm tempted to say something douchey like 'It was well past time,' but I won't."

She gently thumped his chest with her fist. "Gosh, I appreciate that. Such a gentleman. Seriously, though…"

His arm around her felt good, somehow protective, emphasizing the connection between them. In a way, it was as though a weight had been lifted. She no longer struggled with the uncertainty of their status. It was definite at last. It was *real*.

In a soft voice, she said, "I gotta admit, it was probably overdue. And now, well, at least we know what's up. We're together. 'An item' or whatever cheesy way people have of putting it."

"That would be correct. Oh," he remarked, an almost sly look on his handsome face, "I'd thought about it before. *Long* before. And more times than I can remember. But if you've learned anything about men, I'm sure that doesn't shock you."

"I have," she riposted, "and it doesn't. Buncha animals, even though I'm the one who turns into a goddamn wolf and you don't."

He nodded, and his smirk cracked into open laughter. "Quite the irony. Oh, you did fine, by the way. Nothing to be ashamed of in that department."

She stopped and put her hands on her hips, looking squarely at him. "Just *fine*, huh?"

He pouted innocently. "Well, maybe more like 'good.' I mean, there's always room for improvement, but don't worry, you're off to a great start. You just need more practice. The more and sooner, the better."

She blushed. "Let's see how things are looking in town. Got to make sure the witches haven't blown half the place up. If not, then yeah. I'd definitely be open to more practice."

"Sounds like a plan." One of his hands descended behind her and squeezed her butt.

She jumped, a shiver going through her, and blushed harder. "Hey, now. Watch yourself, boy. We're almost in my backyard where my brothers might see. Have *some* decency, you filthy heathen."

He retracted his hand but quipped, "I have *plenty* of decency."

They came to the Nordin property and were only seven steps into the yard when the back door opened and Jacob leaned out, taking them in at a glance.

"Welcome back," he called. "You probably just want to sit down and eat as usual, but there's some stuff going on you oughta know about."

Bailey tensed, and it must have shown since her brother held up a hand.

"Nothing terrible. Not yet, anyway. In fact, it's probably a good thing. Lots of new Weres rolling into town. People we haven't seen or heard of, a few loners plus obscure packs from around the state, and even a few from Washington and Idaho."

The werewitch and the wizard exchanged surprised glances.

"Yeah," Bailey returned, "I'd say that's a good thing under the present circumstances. How many? Weres, I mean, rather than packs."

Jacob shrugged. "I dunno. At least thirty, maybe more

like fifty. You're going into town today, right? We can figure it out then."

Roland raised a finger. "What's for breakfast?"

The eldest Nordin brother made a sour face. "Uh, coffee, I guess. We haven't made anything. Kurt's sleeping, and Russell joined one of the patrols. I kinda wanted to go with him, honestly, but we felt like someone ought to be here to hold the fort."

Roland pouted, but Bailey waved a hand in front of his face and spoke for both of them. "That's fine. I just hope Russell knows what he's doing."

It almost made her sick, imagining him being the first one to stumble onto the next wave of Venatori and incurring their wrath. Then again, even without magic, he was about as tough as werewolves came.

Jacob held the door as they walked in. "We all know what we're doing now," he retorted. "Defending our damn town."

They relaxed for fifteen or twenty minutes and had a cup of coffee. Jacob had made it himself, so it was strong, though not on the same level as Russell's.

After a short period of conversation about how Sheriff Browne had deputized four or five more citizens and their father was rushing back to help with things, Bailey made her decision about what to do today.

"So," she began, "I think Roland and me *do* need a proper breakfast, and like you said, we should go into town and meet the new guys anyway. Let's go get something to eat at the Elk and, uh, do a round of inspection of the defenses while we're at it. Hell, I sound like a colonel or something."

Roland stretched his arms. "Good idea. Let's take a shower first, though. If we do get into another battle, we'll be sweating even *more*."

Bailey pretended to ignore the implication. "Yeah. You go ahead and take yours first, and I'll take mine right after."

He gave her a disappointed look but didn't protest. Bailey wasn't about to do anything that would give her brothers more cause to make fun of her.

Soon they were in her Tundra and rolling down Greenhearth's main street toward the diner. It seemed like there were fewer people out doing normal things, which broke her heart. She hated the thought that the locals were afraid to live their lives as usual. But there were plenty of Weres, as well as sporadic humans, walking around in small groups and keeping an eye on things.

A few of them waved as she passed. "Well," she commented, "people are enthusiastic about the project, anyway."

"Indeed," said Roland. "When the sheriff's station gets a wall blown out and one of the local cops gets killed, that's usually something to pay attention to."

When they arrived at the diner, it was bustling, though more with lycanthropes than with the human regulars. Again, Bailey worried about how the locals would react to all this.

It's a temporary situation, she told herself. *We're doing what we must to protect the whole community. Soon this will be over, and everything will be back to normal.*

Cheryl greeted them just inside the door. "Oh, hi, Bailey. And Roland. You having breakfast?" She seemed subtly nervous, but at least she was making an effort to be friendly.

"Affirmative," Bailey replied. "This dipshit complained when my brothers didn't cook for him for once, so I had no choice."

"Hey!" Roland protested. "I'm not complaining about eating here, either. Might even be better. And at least they made coffee."

The pair drew the eyes of various newcomers as they walked past, and when Cheryl led them into the dining room, it looked as though a meeting or conference was going on. All werewolves, and only about half of them were familiar. They beckoned, and Cheryl gave them a table near the center of the crowd.

Will Waldsbach greeted her first. "Bailey. I'm the South Cliff alpha now, with the Oberlins forced out. You're kind of a celebrity these days. Most of these guys have heard about what's going on. Everyone in our corner of the US knows what the Venatori have been doing and that you've been kicking ass and taking names."

She and Roland were suddenly surrounded, mostly by young men, leading representatives of the new packs Jacob had mentioned and even a couple of packless outcasts, regional drifters who'd barely acknowledged their Were heritage until now. There was an intensity in their eyes, but not the threatening kind.

They'd all come to declare their support for the new shaman.

A towering, gaunt-faced man from somewhere down in the southeast corner of Oregon put a fist over his heart. "You have our allegiance," he stated. "Fenris put his word behind you, and you've done a lot to protect our kind. If those witches think they can wipe us out, they're going to have to try harder."

Another warrior, short and pudgy but still formidable with his thick muscles and cantankerous face, concurred. "After you rescued the girls in Seattle, we made a note of your name. We helped point the cops toward the assholes responsible for that. With this going on, we're glad we remembered you. My boys and I will be staying around town as long as you need us."

Others stepped in and made similar statements. It was overwhelming, and Bailey flushed with pride and gratitude. She tried not to let it go to her head. They were here because a terrible thing was happening, and it was her duty to lead them wisely and ensure the overall well-being of wolfdom. She couldn't betray their trust by acting like a rock star or abusing her power.

"Thank you," she said at the end. "I…damn. Honestly, I can't tell you all how much it means to me to hear this. I used to feel like I didn't fit in with Weres in general, and now, well, that's definitely not the case."

She smiled and looked down at the table to gather her thoughts before addressing them again. "But this isn't about me at the end of the day. It's about you, and about all of us. And the people of Greenhearth—the regular humans who've been our friends since forever, and who I'd protect the same as my own family."

Some of those humans, she knew, were dining in the corners and overheard her. If they spread the word, it would help calm some of the tensions that had arisen lately.

The pack leaders—some alphas, some shamans, some warrior-lieutenants acting on behalf of their alphas back home—agreed and reaffirmed their allegiance, then offered to take Bailey out to meet the rest of their people and learn how all the sentries were positioned.

She agreed, overjoyed even as their loyalty humbled her.

The gaunt-faced man from the southeast looked at Roland and placed a massive hand on his shoulder. The wizard, absorbed in sipping coffee, raised his eyebrows and waited for him to speak.

"And you," the Were rumbled. "We've heard of you also, Roland. You're not our kind, but you've helped through all of this. If Bailey trusts you, then so do we."

"Thanks," Roland quipped. "I try."

Bailey rubbed her foot against his lower leg under the table. She wondered if she ought to make some sort of announcement about them being in a relationship at last, but there was someone she wanted to talk to first.

The Tundra pulled in at the auto shop, where life and the business of fixing cars went on as usual, even with a small army of werewolves patrolling the town in case of a witch invasion. People needed to drive, after all.

Bailey and Roland hopped down from the truck and strode toward the repair bays, where Gunney and the rest of his crew were hard at work on a rusted white minivan and a red Dodge Charger LX. The crusty old head mechanic noted their approach with a short glance, then returned to writing something on a clipboard, waiting for them to come to him.

"Hi, Gunney." Bailey waved. "Obviously we're okay, and so are you."

Roland fidgeted. "I think I drank a bit too much coffee, though."

The older man looked at her, ignoring the wizard for the moment. "That we are. Lot of newcomers around town, but they're your people, near as I can tell. Look like real hardasses in some cases too, which has some of the locals a little jumpy, but hardasses are just what we need these days. Assuming they're on our side."

She nodded. "Yeah, that's the idea. And they…well, they pledged loyalty to me." For a second she grinned, but it turned into a lengthy sigh. "I gotta make sure I don't disappoint them or screw up."

Gunney flipped his cap off his head, airing out his scalp and letting his hair spill out for a moment before returning the hat to its usual place.

"Hey, now, remember what I told you. One thing at a time and you'll do fine. Besides, you're probably the best woman for the job of keeping us all from being turned into toads or stuck in some fuckin' cauldron or whatever. Christ, I thought I'd seen some shit, but things just keep getting crazier around here."

Roland nodded. "That's one way of putting it."

"Yeah, well," Bailey added, "we just wanted to see how you're doing. I'd stay and help, but I have to make sure everyone's on their shit. This whole valley is a target. No sugarcoating it."

The aging mechanic grimaced but wasn't about to argue.

"Anyhow, come along out back. There's something I want to show you."

Bailey raised her eyebrows. "Oh, really?" She had a suspicion as to what it might be but kept her mouth shut so he could surprise her.

"Um," Roland interjected, "I *really* need to use the bathroom, so I'll leave you guys to it."

Gunney waved a hand. "Yeah, help yourself. You know where it's at."

He and Bailey tramped through the dirt lot behind the shop toward the yard where the old man kept his spare cars, spare parts, and personal projects. It was the home of his beloved Trans Am, among other less illustrious things.

Bailey waited just outside the yard as Gunney went in, fired up an engine, and drove out the Camaro she'd helped him work on recently. He parked it right in front of her and stepped out.

He inhaled and looked at the car. "It isn't fully restored yet, just matte gray with primer, but that can be amended when there's time. It's drivable, though. And," he turned to look at her, "more importantly, it's yours. Permanently, I mean."

Her jaw dropped. She'd figured that he wanted to show her the Camaro, but she hadn't expected *this*. "Damn, Gunney. I...don't know what to say. Except thanks, obviously."

Grinning openly, he tossed her the keys. "Consider it a gift after all your years of helping me out, including times you stayed late and worked for free just for the hell of it. I'd say you more than earned it."

She caught the keys in midair, and he folded his arms over his chest and took on a contemplative expression.

"But," he added, "I don't think even you racked up enough goodwill to get the Trans Am. That thing's still mine. No way in *hell* anyone else is getting it."

Bailey laughed and threw her arms around his neck, almost causing him to lose his balance.

"I wouldn't take your Trans Am away from you. I was damn near sick, trying to keep it from getting wrecked in Seattle. And a Camaro is more than enough for me right now. Shit!"

"Just don't let your brothers pressure you about what color to get it done," he advised. "That's up to you."

"Right," she agreed. "Kurt would probably want puce or lime green striped with hot pink or some crap like that 'cause he thinks it'd be funny. I'm thinking either the classic red or something more subdued, like black or dark blue. I dunno. I'll ask Roland."

The girl glanced back and saw that the wizard had emerged from the restroom and was standing by the pit with his hands in his pockets, probably talking to the disembodied voice of Kevin. She turned back to Gunney.

"Oh," she added in a lower voice and tried not to blush. She'd been doing too much of that just lately. "Um, I wanted to tell you, not that it's gonna come as much of a shock, I'm sure, but Roland and I are, you know, *official* now."

He didn't react for a second or two. Then his face, so tough and yet so kindly at the same time, slowly split into a smile that was deeply warm and affectionate, yet somehow sad. His eyes seemed to crinkle.

"Well, I'm happy for you," he said in a soft voice. "He's a good young man. A little…I dunno, *slick* for my taste, but it's not his fault he's from fuckin' Seattle. You two clearly get along, and he's been with you through all this shit. Stayed by your side and watched your back the whole time, even with the world blowing up. Not a lot of guys would've done that. Bailey…"

He reached out a leathery hand and placed it on her soft cheek. "I want you to be happy. You're the daughter I never had. No offense to your father, of course, but well, you know what I mean."

"I do," she shot back quickly, swallowing past a sudden lump in her throat. She grabbed him and hugged him for a second time.

After a moment, Roland started to wander over, and Bailey released the old man. She spun the keys around her forefinger.

"Okay, then," she proclaimed, "time for a test drive. Is it okay if I leave the Tundra here?"

He nodded. "Sure, just bring it around back if you're gonna be gone for more than a few minutes so you're not blocking anyone out front."

"Deal."

A local construction company had given the sheriff a discount on repairs to the building, and volunteers from the church had also lent a hand. When Bailey and Roland pulled up in her new car, the ravaged back wall was mostly replaced, although they weren't putting a window in this time. The rest of the station still had burn scars and other minor or cosmetic damage, but it was structurally sound.

Browne came out to greet them as they got out. He was still walking with a cane. His Magnum was holstered at his side, and he had a loaded hunting rifle slung over his back.

Bailey wondered if he could shoot straight from a standing position with his side and leg injured like that, but he was as tough as anyone else in Greenhearth.

She waved. "Morning, Sheriff. Thought we'd check and see how things are going. So far, it's been quiet in town."

He gave a curt nod. "Yes, it has. Almost too quiet. The main repairs are just about done. Smolinski's fine. I'm trying to get the new deputies up to speed, although they're men with decent heads on their shoulders who at least know how to shoot straight. Jurgensen's funeral is in two days."

Bailey bowed her head. The sheriff had relayed the last bit of information in the same even-toned, no-nonsense way as the other tidbits. That was how he was, but she knew he was even more torn up inside than she was. Jurgensen had served the town for almost twenty years.

"I'll attend," she stated. "Is it okay if I come in?"

Again he nodded, more by thrusting out his chin than anything else. "Sure. Just watch your step."

Roland came along as she followed Browne into the lobby. The front doors had been replaced as well. The crude metal looked like hell, but at least it would function and offer halfway decent protection.

Within, the building had the typical look, feel, and smell

of a structure undergoing renovations. Tarps, raw plaster, dust, and cans of sealant were everywhere.

The sheriff informed them of a couple more things as they walked toward the back room where the witch Rhona had briefly been held.

"Still no word from our mysterious friends in the federal government," he said. "They probably have another thousand or so forms to fill out before they can set foot in town, just in case someone's jurisdictional toes get stepped on."

Roland frowned. "Could be. Usually they can override other agencies and departments, from what I've heard, but the scale and scope of what's going on might be what's causing the delay."

Browne glanced at the wizard, then resumed his slow trek. "We'll see. They ought to at least return my calls. I'm on the cusp of calling in help from other towns, even if it would be the kind of help that, shall we say, would be surprised to learn what we've got going on."

The wizard snapped his fingers. "You should tell that to the Agency. Their primary purpose is to contain all knowledge of the supernatural, so the threat of outsiders finding out there's a gang war between shapeshifters and spellcasters might light a fire under their asses."

"I did," said Browne, "but thanks for the advice."

They came to the rear chamber, where Smolinski was monitoring some kind of radar-type device while a workman outside painted the new wall. There was still a small hole in it near the top. They'd run out of material and would plug the gap later.

The deputy sighed. "Nothing. I wonder if they're trying

to freak us out by making us wait as long as possible. Psychological warfare and all that."

Rather than responding to the comment, the sheriff turned to Bailey. "Where's your friend Marcus? Haven't seen him lately."

"I'm not sure," she answered. "He comes and goes. It'd be good to have him around, though." Then she remembered what he'd said at the memorial service—that he couldn't directly intervene without drawing too much attention to them all. Images of Freya and Baldur popped into her head.

Something changed in the air. It was subtle, like a shifting of electromagnetic current or a drop in air pressure when one drives up a steep mountainside, and the light overhead flickered.

Roland tensed, blinking and looking around.

Bailey felt her gut clench; something was wrong. "What is it?"

"A spell," he replied in a hurry. "It was latent in here the whole time, but they masked it well. A trigger that would go off like a silent alarm when we returned and weren't on our guard. It's tied to the consciousness of the witch who cast it—that Rhona chick—so she must still be alive. And she has to be able to see the vicinity of where the trigger is located."

Sheriff Browne's eyes slowly widened. "They're here."

Bailey bolted back down the hall toward the front entrance.

"Bailey!" Roland cried out. "Get back here. It's too dangerous! For fuck's sake!" His feet pounded the floor behind her.

She'd already reached the door and flung it open, her left hand prepared to cast a shield spell at an instant's notice, her eyes and other senses searching everywhere at once.

The streets were lined with female shapes, most clad in distinctive outfits of dark leather, although some were in normal civilian clothes, all of them facing toward the sheriff's station. They were positioned in clusters at strategic vantage points throughout the town. Quite a few of them stood on the roofs of nearby buildings. It was as though all had winked into existence within the last minute or two.

Bailey didn't know how many might be behind the station, blocked from sight as they were, but judging by what she could see, there had to be at least fifty witches in total. Her jaw slowly fell open.

Standing on the roof of the store across the street, gazing straight at her, were two who stood out. One was Rhona, grinning in a vicious, shark-like way. Her trap had worked, and she was looking forward to revenge.

The other had to be the leader of the expedition—a tall woman with strawberry-blonde hair who radiated power.

"Fuck," Bailey muttered as Roland came up beside her.

Wolves howled and the patrolling packs and sentries rushed toward their enemies, their shock giving way to rage.

Rhona waved. "What is the matter? You look so surprised!"

The redhead beside her flicked her fingers. "This might be a *proper* fight for once," she said in what sounded like a Scottish accent, her voice magnified to echo throughout the valley. "Kill every last one of the werewolves. Flatten the whole bloody town if you have to."

Although she knew they'd block it, Bailey hurled a beam of burning plasma toward the pair atop the store. Then she slammed the door shut as all hell broke loose. Roland had already covered the front of the station with a glowing green shield.

"Well," he remarked as screams and crashes and crackles of fire and electricity raged outside, "this is bad, don't you think? Where's a god when you need one?"

Something exploded outside the door and the front windows shattered, smoking chunks of asphalt and concrete flying in to scatter across the floor.

Bailey gritted her teeth. "We *don't* need one! My Weres can take them out, and I'm personally gonna dismantle those bitches!"

Outside, lupine howls transformed into screams of agony as things burned and shattered, and the handful of cops in the station readied their guns.

CHAPTER SIXTEEN

So much happened so quickly that Bailey, acting mostly on instinct and reflex, could barely keep her conscious mind up with it all. It seemed as though time had slowed down to accommodate the sheer volume of chaos and violence that had erupted.

Bailey ran from one end of the station to the other more times than she could count in a couple of minutes. Out front, the windows were blown out, and she poked her head and arms through them just long enough to throw deadly spells at the witches outside, barely avoiding their counterattacks each time.

In back, the sorceresses had found the weak point near the repaired wall and blasted it apart again, undoing the days of labor it had taken to fix it. Far worse, the poor construction guy who'd been finishing up the job lay dead outside, his body torn up and smoking from plasma spears or lightning.

The cops were all firing through the door-sized hole in

the wall. A single witch lay dead as well, out in the street where they huddled, but there were far more where she'd come from. Bailey sent a wave of ice-cold wind in that direction, hoping to slow or disorient the attackers enough for Browne and his men to fight back.

Then she was out front again, helping to bolster Roland's shield and aiding him in tossing arcane counteroffensive measures toward the women in the road or on the surrounding roofs.

"This isn't working," Bailey protested. "We can't defend this building with that many of them positioned above us. I'm going out. I'm the one they want anyway."

Outside, she could hear the bestial sounds of lycanthropic attacks hitting home—heavy bodies moving at speed, snarls, and thrashing. The Weres were doing their part, but they were having to break through the thick circle of witches, cut off from Bailey, Roland, and the officers.

The station was a trap, and they'd sprung it.

"Bullshit!" Roland frothed. "If you go out there, you're going to be dead in, like, eight seconds."

"No," she stated. "I'll be *past* them in *four* seconds. Then I'll lead a charge of Weres, and we'll break their fuckin' lines down the middle and regroup with you guys."

Not waiting for his response, she shifted into wolf form and jumped out the window.

Unsurprisingly, ten or more blasts of magic converged on her the second she was outside, but she'd expected as much and had shielded herself. Through great force of will, she even made it colorless, so it took the witches a moment to realize she *was* shielded. Their attacks were deflected, stalled, or fizzled out before they touched her.

With powerful leaps, she landed on top of the nearby bank, scattering a couple of the Venatori who'd taken positions there, then moved across other roofs, interrupting the activities of the witches on them, and in one case even knocking a sorceress off. She fell screaming and flailing onto a parking meter, breaking her spine and spilling blood on the sidewalk.

Then she was past the skirmish line, and half a dozen wolves were converging on her position. It had taken six seconds rather than four, but close enough.

Still in beast form, she growled at the lycanthropes who'd rallied to her and motioned for them to go back the way she'd come. Snarling with rising bloodlust, they followed, and together they smashed into the Venatori line from the rear.

Elemental and arcane magic flew in all directions, Bailey blocking or redirecting it where she could. One of her Weres fell dead, but the others trampled or ravaged a cluster of witches before them, the bodies rolling through the streets. Then they loped toward the sheriff's station.

As Bailey passed, the apparent leader of the witches, with Rhona at her side, jumped down from their perch, drifting softly to the asphalt near the center of town and drawing their allies closer to them. The Scottish woman gestured, and two parked cars shot into the air and then rocketed toward the wolves.

Most of them scattered in time to avoid the one, while Bailey magically caught the other in midair, set it on fire, and then dropped it on her foes. The commander stopped it mere feet from herself and instead chucked it a quarter-mile behind her toward a group of wolves who'd come from that direction. The flaming wreck crushed at least two of them.

"Goddammit," Bailey raged, changing back to human. "You guys circle around them. Draw fire and strike when you can, but don't risk yourselves. We need more Weres fighting together."

Looking around, she realized that while the majority of the enemy were grouped in the middle of Greenhearth, other small groups of witches were prowling around the edge of the town, acting as skirmishers and harriers, preventing many of the werewolves from joining the main battle.

On the plus side, Roland, Browne, and the deputies had grouped together near the front door of the station, well-protected by the wizard's shields.

There were three Weres approaching the melee from a side street. A single witch appeared behind them, drawing their attention with minor electrical shocks, and they turned to attack her.

"No!" Bailey cried, running, still in human form but magically boosting her speed and distance, to cover them from behind.

A storm of magic came from the central coven. It would have incinerated them all had Bailey not conjured a shield at the last instant, which she combined with a telekinetic reflective force that turned half the deadly mass back on its casters. Witches dodged or blocked, with one failing to do so. Lightning, fire, plasma, and acid engulfed her, and she fell apart in a mass of blackened bones.

The three Weres she'd just saved looked at Bailey with

wide eyes. They'd killed the witch who'd distracted them, but they knew they owed her their lives. She motioned them on, telling them to fight smarter.

For a moment, as wolves converged on the battle and started acting according to strategy, it seemed like Green-hearth might be getting the upper hand over the Order's troops. That was when Marcus stepped out of the shadows beside Bailey as she paused for a second's rest.

"Can you help?" she asked immediately.

He shook his head. "I cannot. Not directly, anyway, without bringing the wrath of the other gods down on us all. We don't want that. But…"

He opened a portal behind him and seven or eight werewolves streamed out, falling upon a formation of witches who'd moved toward Bailey in a growling, thrashing mass.

"…I was able to recruit more warriors to our cause." The god smiled sardonically.

Bailey breathed. "Better than nothing."

"And," Fenris added, "I saw you risk yourself to save those three a moment ago. You're doing exactly what you need to. Keep fighting and keep leading!"

Then he was gone.

Bailey rejoined the battle. The moment of their community's advantage was brief, however.

At the four points of a square around the town center, glowing amethyst portals opened and out poured witches. Two leather-clad Venatori emerged from each, and following them were other non-Order witches, ranging in number from two to six—local sorceresses they had recruited to their cause, brought in as reinforcements to the already massive force of witches assaulting the town.

Bailey motioned four big Weres over to her. "We're gonna charge those new arrivals," she said. "Take out the ones in the leather catsuits first. They're stronger and more dangerous. I'll lead since I'm the one they want most. It'll draw most of the fire away from you guys. Got it?"

They did. Taking a deep breath, Bailey shifted again into her wolf form, then bounded toward the cluster of smirking women near the closest of the purple doorways.

She narrowly dodged a fireball, then crashed into one of the two Venatori, a pair of the Weres with her attacking the other while the remaining two wolves pounced on the lesser witches.

One of the lycanthropes took a nasty burn on the hip and leg, inhibiting his ability to run or pounce, but he could walk stealthy enough to act as a lookout or lie in ambush. As for the witches, all lay dead and bloodied on the street.

"We lost the element of surprise," said Bailey, "so we gotta be more careful with the next group."

This time, she circled around the pack, summoning magic as needed while in her wolf shape to repel or distract the lead witches as her Weres took out the lesser ones. One of them leapt at a Venatori soldier, only to yelp and slump dead to the ground, a magenta plasma-blade stuck through his mouth and out the back of his skull.

Bailey roared and pounced on the witch, ripping her head off in retaliation and spitting it out. The remaining non-Order sorceress fled screaming toward the main group near the Scottish leader.

Bailey saw that the Venatori controlled most of the town's territory and that far too many lupine forms lay motionless in the streets or against walls, or otherwise torn and burned and blasted beyond all help.

They were slowly losing. They simply didn't have the numbers to repel such a powerful force of invaders. The average witch was a match for the average werewolf, and most of their nemeses were full Venatori, each as powerful as a small coven of lesser channelers.

She sought out Roland and found him still working with the cops who'd emerged from the deathtrap building to protect them from magical attacks while they counterattacked with simple but effective bullets, dropping a witch here and there with well-placed shots.

"Roland!" Bailey called. "I'm sorry, but we need to do this together with magic. My wolves can only do so much."

"Do it *here*, then," he demanded, gritting his teeth as he tried to repel five different kinds of arcane blasts at once and also struggled against unseen waves of fear, despair and confusion. "If I leave this spot, these guys are all going to die."

The cops and deputies clearly heard him but they didn't react, focused as they were on firing, taking cover behind streetlights or piles of rubble, and reloading.

Bailey almost panicked. Anywhere she tried to go to redirect her own efforts, she left someone weaker, while the Venatori seemed just as strong as they'd been at the start of the fight.

From the sky came a growling, buzzing roar, and Bailey shot a glance at the heavens, expecting something like a lightning storm or a swarm of meteors to descend upon the town. What she saw shocked her to momentary stillness.

Over the mountains came a squadron of black helicopters. At least a dozen, with seven or eight coming from the south, but a couple more from the other three directions, too, all converging on the Hearth Valley.

Roland saw them, too. *"Holy shit!"* he exclaimed, his eyes wild and his sweaty hair flying in the hot breeze. "Gondor called for aid, and the Riders of Rohan came. Hah! Oh, this is great!"

Turning her eyes to the roads leading out of the hills, Bailey saw that the choppers weren't the only vehicles coming into town. Black jeeps and vans streamed in off side roads as well as the main highway. One of them rammed a startled witch and crushed her beneath its wheels.

They came to a stop on the high ground surrounding the town center, then doors opened and men in dark suits and glasses jumped out. All of them held strange silver guns that looked like something aliens in a science fiction movie would wield, and they wasted no time.

Beams of magenta-white arcanoplasm shot into the melee, sending witches scurrying for cover, carving through magic shields, kicking up molten fragments of earth, and in some cases, striking the sorceresses and reducing them to piles of bleached ash.

Will Waldsbach, bloody-faced but alive as he struggled atop the roof of the grocery store, threw up his arms. "Yes! *Yes*, goddammit!" He let out a howl of triumph. Other Weres, scattered around the valley by the violence, echoed him.

The helicopters swept overhead and agents leaned out of doors to fire similar beams from the sky, killing a few more witches and putting others on the defensive. Bailey suddenly realized with a leap of her heart and spirits that the battle was winnable.

Townsend was leading a group of men into the town square area along the highway even now, laying suppressing fire on the main cluster of Venatori who'd surrounded their commander. The witches turned most of their attention to fighting the agents, freeing up the majority of the Weres.

Bailey knew what she had to do. She turned to Roland. "Stay here. Help them," she barked, and then she fell to her hands and knees, already shifting, and leapt over the top of the nearest building to bound through the streets.

With the Agency harassing the main force of sorceresses, Bailey made the rounds, directing her scattered wolves to encircle the town and systematically hunt down and destroy those witches who were positioned away from the central group.

Some of the Venatori and their non-Order patsies fought valiantly, almost arrogantly, as though they refused to believe that the tide had turned. Others panicked and tried to flee.

Most died. The few who tried to surrender Bailey just wounded, biting down on their legs or tossing them hard into walls and leaving them to be rounded up by other Weres. She'd have to trust them to keep watch and the witches not to try to backstab them. There was still the rest of the battle for her to fight.

Magic rained down, and furry shapes pounced. Bodies

dropped. Bailey knew her people were still dying, but with the battle's outcome looking favorable, their sacrifices might well lead to victory. Given that the wolves knew the town and countryside, and using their superior physical abilities, the Venatori were having more trouble pinning them down.

Soon, Weres again controlled the outskirts of the town and the forested slopes of the surrounding foothills, all the peripheral witches having been killed or otherwise neutralized. The main battle between the women in leather and the men in sunglasses still raged at the center of Greenhearth, however. With mounting horror, Bailey saw that agents were starting to soar into the air, clearly not of their own accord, some of them rising half a mile into the sky before plummeting back into the hills, screaming all the while. Cars levitated and smashed down among the men's ranks. It had to be the Scotswoman; Bailey had been able to *feel* her power.

Bailey shifted back to human form. Two wolves stood nearby, waiting for instruction.

"Keep patrolling the edges and pick off any witches you can," she said. "I'm going to help." She set off at a run toward the main battle.

The shortest route lay through an alley between two buildings. Bailey sprinted through it, thinking only of how she could pile magical pressure on the Venatori without hitting any of the agents or getting in the way.

Then she tripped. Something had snagged her ankle, and flailing her arms, she flew straight toward the pavement. Beneath the point of impact, a burbling mass of blackish-purple fluid like a dark melting giant flower suddenly appeared.

"Oh, crap!" she exclaimed as she landed in it. It clung to her limbs and body and hair like glue, and she struggled to turn over enough to see what was going on.

Above her stood Rhona, laughing with glee as her brown braid whipped behind her like a snake's tail. She'd set some kind of invisible tripwire and caught Bailey like an insect on flypaper. A violet plasma-blade grew from her hand.

Then she screamed. Another magical blade, this one emerald, protruded from her chest, and she looked down at it even as her eyes went glassy. Roland tossed her aside and her body slumped, unmoving, against the wall.

"And to think," the wizard gasped, "I was starting to feel like a third wheel."

"Roland, help me get out of this stuff," Bailey urged. "And thanks. I need to get into that battle. It's looking like a stalemate."

Grimacing, he knelt beside her and drew all the moisture out of the strange black substance so that it hardened and then crumbled to dust. She broke through it and struggled back to her feet. Then, together, they charged toward the battle.

Once they were out on the highway, a quarter-mile or less from the edge of the melee, Bailey realized that they might be too late.

The Venatori's commander, grinning hugely as her hair flapped in the breeze, raised both her hands and made another sound-enhanced announcement even as beams and bolts and waves of force streaked around her. Bailey had the disturbing impression that not only was the woman relishing all the violence of combat, but she also enjoyed showing off.

"You men think you're hard," she proclaimed, her voice echoing over the din. "Do you know how old I am? *Thirty-six*. And I sit on the ruling council. You think I got that far that young by being *soft?*"

With a swipe of her hand, the hillside behind her shifted as though an earthquake had struck it. But it wasn't the land moving; it was the trees.

At least two dozen fully-grown pines detached from the slope, their roots torn free of the ground, and flew upwards in an arc, descending toward the lines of the agency's soldiers like colossal green javelins.

"Holy living fuck!" Roland shouted. "Well, she obviously specialized in telekinesis."

The agents fired their alien weapons skyward, destroying some of the trees and sending burning fragments raining down. Without the beams pressing down on the witches, lightning and ice shot out from the ranks of the Venatori toward their foes. Two agents fell dead.

Bailey threw up her arms. "We gotta stop those things!"

Roland was already on it. A huge mass of shimmering green light, the biggest shield he'd ever conjured, spread above the men in black. The trees struck it and slowed but did not stop. Their large mass, combined with the broad area he'd had to cover, made it impossible to keep the shield strong enough to immobilize the projectiles.

Instead, the werewitch reached up with her mind and

grabbed them. One or two at a time, she directed telekinetic force of her own against them, shifting them off-course and causing them to thump into abandoned side streets or fly back toward the hills to crash amidst the forest.

It was all the help the agents needed. Townsend had rushed back to his jeep and come back with what looked like a silver grenade. He pressed a button and tossed it into the mass of the witches, right toward their leader.

The woman's resounding laughter cut off as the bomb detonated. A huge sphere of crackling purple light spread over the sorceresses, ensnaring some of them in a static field that left them immobilized and writhing in pain.

The Venatori leader had already countered, though. A mass of hazy darkness spread from her to the witches nearest her, encompassing and protecting them, and then, her face contorting in a snarl, she whipped a hand in front of her face, and all the women within the gloomy substance vanished with a purple flash.

It was over. The witches' leader had retreated, leaving only the dead and the captives.

Bailey fell to her knees, her arms flying skyward. "Yes! Oh, gods, I can't fucking believe it. We did it. It's over!"

Similar shouts and howls and cheers went up around the valley as Weres and agents and normal humans were overcome with elation and relief. They'd repelled the seemingly insurmountable attack. They still lived.

Roland came up behind the girl as she knelt and put his hands on her shoulders. She leaned her head back against his lower body. He handed her a man's shirt he'd found somewhere.

"You know," he pointed out, "you really should be facing the opposite direction for that."

"Shut up." She laughed. "You'll pay for that later. For now, though…"

She sighed, got to her feet, and put on the shirt, which came almost to her knees, then they walked toward the center of town.

The Agency's personnel, aided by the sheriff and his deputies, were securing the area and detaining the witches who'd been caught in the purple energy field created by the silver grenade. From around the edges of town, Weres dragged other sorceresses they'd wounded or captured.

Sirens blared as a fire truck and a couple of ambulances made for the village's center—not a long drive since Emergency Services was right next to the sheriff's station. Random citizens drifted out of their homes, frightened but slowly realizing the threat had passed.

Townsend greeted the pair. "I told you," he said, resting his silver plasma gun on his shoulder. "I said I'd get through to them eventually. I wish it had been sooner, but it wasn't too late. And we've sent a message, one they'll have no choice but to get."

Roland nodded. "Let's hope they get it good and hard."

Behind Townsend, other agents clapped anti-magic handcuffs on the frazzled witch captives, peppering them with questions and promising them clemency if they cooperated.

Soon, emergency workers began to care for those who needed it, and the Weres who'd fought so bravely congregated around Bailey.

"Thank you for all you've done," she told them. "We've

lost more of our brothers, but it was thanks to our actions that we saved a lot more." Looking around, she saw Russell among the surviving warriors and almost melted with relief. He was spattered with blood, but it didn't seem to be his.

The Weres saluted, the fierce gleam of pride and admiration in their eyes saying more than words could.

Bailey went on, "I gotta help with the cleanup and make sure everyone else is okay."

Roland accompanied her as they returned to the mass of humans. Behind them, the lycanthropes melted into the forest.

Gunney came down to check on them and the Camaro. Parked in the rear corner of a lot just outside the town center, it had somehow survived the miniature apocalypse, much to the relief of both him and Bailey.

Townspeople came by to offer their thanks or congratulations. Occasionally they were livid with residual fear over the fact that this had happened, but on the whole, it seemed that everyone understood what was going on and why.

As Bailey did what she could to aid them all, some put their hands on her shoulder or gave her nods as they passed.

Roland smiled. "I'm starting to think people *like* you. It's not just me, then."

"Yeah, yeah." She grunted as she unloaded a pallet of bottled water the grocery store was donating to the emergency workers from a truck. "They better not get the idea that they're allowed to like me the same way you do, though."

"Damn right," he said, smiling, then planted a quick kiss on her lips.

The hours passed, everyone helping everyone else get to the finish line of a long, hard day. Roland disappeared to join her brothers in cleaning up some wreckage that was blocking the street.

As darkness began to creep over the mountains, Bailey headed off to take a coffee break. She'd been tending wounded townsfolk at a makeshift outdoor clinic they'd set up near the sheriff's office.

Suddenly, a tall figure was standing beside her, having appeared out of nowhere. Again. "Bailey," he said.

She turned to him. "Nice to see you. It would have been even nicer to have had your help. Sorry. People died out there, but we won. Kicked their asses all the way back to France or wherever, I hope."

"Yes," said Fenris. "War has started, whether we wanted it or not, and your people rallied behind you. You commanded them ably and helped your allies as well. The situation may be horrible, but you're handling it. I'm proud of you."

She was embarrassed by the praise. "Thanks. I just… worry. I'm starting to feel like I'm a kid on a slide, just getting to the part where you no longer have the choice to get off; you can only slide down. Does that make sense? I mean, I'm worried that all this means my visions are coming true. There's gonna be more all-out conflict and destruction and death."

She closed her eyes for a moment and admitted to herself that she was afraid of what her god might tell her.

When she looked at him again, his face was unreadable—as usual—in the darkness of his hood.

"We'll just have to wait and see," he stated.

She frowned and looked into the distance at the warm red glow behind the Cascades to the west, then toward the gathering darkness to the east.

"I guess so."

You made it! Here we are again at the end of book 4! Thank you so much for reading this far.

Avoiding the topic of coronavirus since we're living that joy (except to say I hope this finds you and yours well), let's talk about Zoom. I've been having fun with it since all my meetings are now held this way. To maximize my enjoyment, I do things like put donuts and croissants up as backgrounds to taunt my team members. Last week, I put up a background showing a live tropical scene with rolling waves and palm trees, and halfway through the meeting, I found out half my head was gone, due to the magic Zoom performs to put me in the picture. No one thought to mention it (thanks, everyone). Kids, don't try this at home. You need your head, especially in meetings.

There is nothing else to do but drive to get food and work, so drive to get food and coffee I shall! Well, there are hikes in the woods (carefully social distancing from raccoons and squirrels and blue jays), and Empress Josephine gets her daily walkies in the direction of her choice, but nothing that has me interacting with other humans. The drive-through at the semi-local Starbucks (next town up—this *is* rural Oregon) is finally open at times when I can get there again. Hallelujah! My routine is re-established. Fish tacos and flat whites, here I come!

I always thank my advance reader team, but I also want to thank the Early Reader team, the ones who read my stories after they are edited. They catch the oopses and point out any last-minute dichotomies, and as such, they helped make this book (and every book) its best. Couldn't do it without you, folks! Thanks for having my back.

I hope you enjoyed Bailey's and Roland's further adventures. They will be back in the final mega of the series. And if you get a moment, drop me a review, please. Those are the lifeblood of any writer. We appreciate you!

Until next time,
Renée

Renée Jaggér Social

Website:
https://reneejagger.com/

Facebook Here:
https://www.facebook.com/reneejaggerauthor/

The WereWitch Series
Bad Attitude (Book One)
A Bit Aggressive (Book Two)
Too Much Magic (Book Three)
Were War (Book 4)

Coming Soon
Were Rages (Book Five)
God Ender (Book Six)
God Trials (Book Seven)
The Troll Solution (Book Eight)

Callie Hart Series
Thin Ice (Book One)
Cold Blood (Book Two)
Feelings Run Deep (Book Three)